advanc

EMPIRE (

"I'm in love with this daring space opera aswirl with sensuality, galactic politics, and cosmic hunger. Barrett is endlessly inventive, crafting a novella of anime-slick vision and dexterous storytelling. A lyrical, sorcerous kind of sci-fi."
—Hailey Piper, author of *Queen of Teeth*

"Grand in scope and brimming with political intrigue, *Empire of the Feast* is a space opera in the truest sense of the term. With lush and sensuous prose, Barrett has created a fully realized world that lingers in the imagination long after you've turned the last page."
—Victor Manibo, author of *The Sleepless*

"An utterly intoxicating blend of sex magic, space politics, and the ravenous void, *Empire of the Feast* is a rare, delicious treat."
—Leigh Harlen, author of *Queens of Noise*

"This novella *fucks* first and foremost. It fucks with your conception of what a book with 'Empire' in the title is going to be about and it definitely fucks with feverish sweat and twisted limb, shuddering sighs and feral climaxes. Barrett hooks the reader immediately with both trenchant narrative and intriguing worldbuilding that are so defiantly interwoven that they may as well be wrought of the same cloth...or fuck tarp. You get what I am saying. Buy this book...and maybe a second copy...you know, for *reasons*."
—Jordan Shiveley, author of *Hot Singles In Your Area*

Neon Hemlock Press
www.neonhemlock.com
@neonhemlock

© 2022 Bendi Barrett

Empire of the Feast
Bendi Barrett

Cover and Interior Design by dave ring
Edited by dave ring
Inside Cover Illustration by Nero Villagallos O'Reilly
Interior Station Illustration by Matthew Spencer

Print ISBN-13: 978-1-952086-44-1
Ebook ISBN-13: 978-1-952086-45-8

Bendi Barrett
EMPIRE OF THE FEAST

Neon Hemlock Press

THE 2022 NEON HEMLOCK NOVELLA SERIES

Empire
of the Feast

BY BENDI BARRETT

For Kevin, who gave me permission to snatch stars from the sky.

ACT I

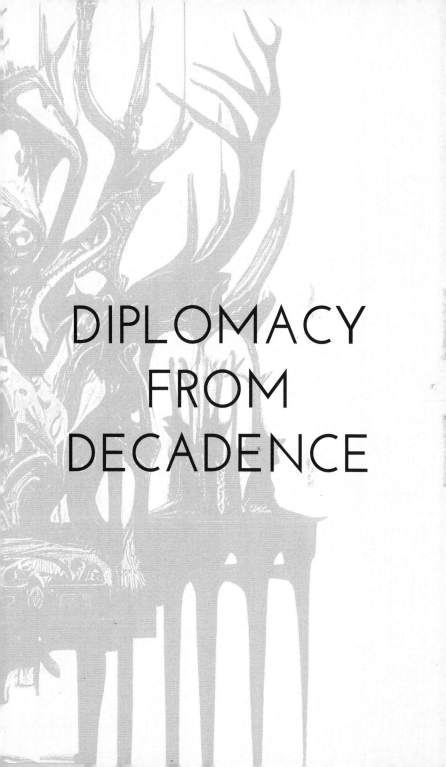

DIPLOMACY
FROM
DECADENCE

IT STARTS LIKE many stories—either noble or perverse—with a bang. And after the cordite flash and the slowing of blood, comes the thought: *Ah. So, it's death. Again.*

This moment of bemused consideration erupts into a searing heat which melts into a stillness so total that it feels as though the syrup-thick viscosity of time won't ever pierce it. Of course, this is a fallacy: time will never be denied.

"Empress?" says a voice, later.

"Empress?" asks the subject back to the querent.

"Ah, so the transfer is complete. Welcome back to the Corrected Center, my liege. The assassin used a piece of truly ancient weaponry; it has since been banned from every world under your beneficent aegis."

The body belonging to the second speaker opens its eyes and takes a first, labored breath. The body's lungs are strong, but its nerves are jittery and its gaze flits around the room.

Room is an understatement so vast that it almost constitutes a lie; the cavernous space is sumptuously appointed with a bed that could sleep a small army, a bar so stocked with vices that it could double as an alchemist's atelier, and a wardrobe fit for…well, an empress. The distance from floor to ceiling is more than twelve times a person's height, its walls curving upward and consisting of perfectly triangular elements. A geodesic dome.

Beyond the walls is space—vast, uncompromising—but worse still is the sun. It is far too close.

The second body screams.

"Empress?" asks the first. "Are you entirely well? Usually, the transfer doesn't leave you so…disorganized." This last word is said with a measure of distaste.

The second looks back at the speaker, takes in the sight: tall and lean with a kindly face and head full of curls, one side a shimmering cerulean and the other a cinnamon red. Skin pale as fatless milk, eyes dark as the void. They're leaning forward now, inspecting the second closely.

"Empress? I…why do you keep calling me that?"

The standing speaker straightens slowly. "An incomplete incarnation? It failed? Problematic. The beast must have had a hand in this and the consequences…no. All things are made possible through the Feast-Empress." A steadying smile is pushed across the tall person's face by main force. "Empress, I am Leeds. Your First-Retainer. And you are the Thirty-Second Feast-Empress *Locum Tenens* of the Staghead Empire. We are in the Corrected Center of the galaxy, a station—naturally—that orbits the Accursed Sun. Does this spark recollection? Can you stand?"

The second can and does, looks around and finally sees the bodies. One is dressed in dark clothing, face down on the ground, with a dire-looking wound in their back that roughly matches the blade at Leeds's side. But the other body…

"That's me, isn't it?"

"Unfortunately, yes. It was an assassination attempt, Empress. A successful one at that. I was seconds too late, and you were killed. Of course, through the river you were reformed to resume your charge. On that note, Empress…"

The body's eyes stare toward the ceiling. A simple golden coronet sits upon her long kinky hair, smooth-edged, but bold against the darkness of her curls. Her skin is dark as well, her lips are full, and the irises of her open, dead eyes are a vicious pink. It brings to mind blood, only slightly diluted, or a besieged ember steadfastly refusing to go out.

"I was murdered."

Leeds, already onto something else, takes a deep breath. "Indeed, Empress. We take great care, but it does sometimes happen. Your empire is vast and its mechanisms legion. Occasionally a murder slips through. But you needn't worry. Empress?"

The second crouches next to their own dead body and lowers the eyelids over those disconcerting eyes, knowing that theirs are the same.

"Emperor," says the second quietly, but firmly.

"Emperor," repeats Leeds slowly. "I see. The river has brought us a son then. How surprising! Though, perhaps not completely auspicious. Some might say that continuity is of grave importance in these times, so a male heir might…well. Apologies, hail and well-met river's son Thirty-Two, Feast-*Emperor* of the Staghead Galaxy."

"Riverson," the emperor rolls the word around his new mouth. "It's as good a name as any."

Leeds goes to one knee and Riverson stands. He forces himself to take his eyes off of his former vessel's body. On his second scan of the room, he takes more in.

Two enormous vertical tapestries hang from the metal rafters. One bears a black-eyed stag staring straight toward the viewer on a green and black striped background; the second is an enormous sun. Strangely, there's a black seam stitched directly through the center of the blazing sphere at a jagged angle. Something about that fissure makes Riverson's stomach lurch.

"What is it that I do here?"

Having been addressed, Leeds rises smoothly. "You govern, my liege. The Corrected Center is a station that orbits this galaxy's sun and functions as the locus of the Staghead Empire, which spans the entire system: more than three thousand worlds, many inhabitable, and full of resources. Your adoring people number in the trillions."

"Except the one who just killed me," Riverson replies.

"Perfect love is aspirational, my liege," Leeds says, then swiftly buries the comment in a torrent of information. "Your previous...liquidation...has put you behind schedule, Emperor Riverson. The Feast will demand your attention, no doubt. But there are also the galactic forces to be seen to: the Luperci envoy will want to confirm your safety, a member of the Perpetual Front is en route to the Corrected Center as we speak for an audience set up by your previous incarnation, and an official of the Cloud's End cult is waiting for an audience."

Leeds recites these appointments without referring to notes of any sort. Their hands are clasped behind their back, their gaze trained squarely on the emperor, while the ruler pads naked across the plush crimson carpet of his private quarters. Riverson is temporarily lost in the pleasure of striding barefoot across the soft carpeting, but he forces himself to focus.

"I've just been murdered, and you want me to attend a feast?" Riverson asks. "What kind of empire are we running?"

"Ah. I see the source of confusion. Not, *a* feast, my liege, *the* Feast. The namesake of your office. The Feast is the mechanism by which the Staghead Empire asserts dominance over the Beast. It's a sort of leash and the source of the river, from which much of the empire's magical bounty flows." Leeds gestures to the sun, burning outside, but Riverson doesn't want to look. He feels *something* in his chest when he looks at it, something like mutual antipathy. Noting his hesitance, Leeds continues a beat later. "For all the gifts of the Staghead Empire, there are certain responsibilities that must be fulfilled lest we risk the ire of a force that dwarfs even your own majesty, my liege."

Riverson raises an eyebrow. "We have to placate…the sun?"

"No, lord," Leeds says. They pause momentarily, seeming to take in the emperor's tabula rasa state, but then continue quickly instead of sitting with the implications. "We placate that which inhabits it. A force that not only survives the incomprehensible heat, but slumbers within it. A slumber that we feed and pray never breaks. Within our sun is the Rapacious and its hungers."

A coolness seizes Riverson, and he thinks, belatedly, of his nakedness. Leeds sees him shiver and hurries to one of the room's half dozen cabinets to retrieve a shimmering cloak that alternates between silver and gold depending on the exact cast of the light. Riverson throws it over his shoulder; thus armored he turns and regards the sun.

The thick transparent panels that form the walls of the dome must shield them from the effects of concentrated sunlight, because Riverson is able to look at the sun directly. As he stares, the patterns of the sun, so abstract and lawless, begin to cohere, almost seem to *call* to him…

"…and of course, there will have to be some recompense. Emperor?"

"What? Yes, I'm sorry, I was…the sun…"

"I would not recommend staring overlong, my liege. The Feast-Emperor has a more specific and sensitive relationship to the thing within the sun than most. In fact, if I were to hazard a guess, it might be that very relationship that has caused your recent memory loss.

"The rituals responsible for your reincarnations are impossibly complex, and require as an energy source the Rapacious itself. These rituals give you endless life and through you give the empire an unbroken line of arcane knowledge and political cunning. So, you are the steward and beneficiary of the monster's incarceration, but it is an ageless beast. An enigmatic, fickle force. You should fear it. We all do."

Riverson hears the awe-struck note in Leeds's voice as they speak about the creature of appetite living in the sun. "So, I'm to be a jailer."

"You are to be the center of everything, lord," Leeds says brightly.

Riverson takes a final glance at the sun and then averts his eyes. He also keeps his gaze from the dead bodies. A few moments of life and already the things he must ignore are stacking.

"You were saying something, Leeds?"

"Right. Recompense. At the moment of your death, a message was sent out to the various political factions that pledge loyalty to the throne. They will all be looking now to the first moments of your re-ascendancy. The assassination must be avenged. We do not know the exact culprits, but there are probable suspects. As such, your likeliest course of action would be the eradication of one of the minor planets that have been attempting to foment rebellion. If you would but give your verbal agreement?" Leeds produces a flat pane of glass that lights up at their touch and with their fingertip swirls a signature and waits.

"Excuse me, *what*?" Riverson replies.

"Lord, this is very much in line with imperial doctrine, as dictated by yourself: Isolate dissenters. Break them. Furthermore, by the standards of production this is a backwater. Small, unexceptional. A few million souls. The empire won't miss it."

"Let me get this straight: you want to implode a *planet* as justice without trial, with no sense of whether any of those people were involved in this." Riverson sweeps a hand to encompass the bodies lying on the ground; seeing his own body throws him into a fit of sudden vertigo. He tries to force himself to look, to see the potential risks of his new life in three dimensions, but sick rises in the back of his throat and his gaze retreats back to the cool, unaffected Leeds.

"Forgiveness, your effulgence, but they are already guilty. They have decided to rebel, and they have not been stopped by their own. Whether or not they are guilty of this crime, they have broken the simplest of covenants: *loyalty to the Corrected Center is absolute*." Leeds softens, but even this softness feels like a calculation. "As your memories are elsewhere at present, allow me to be your record: for hundreds of thousands of years there was strife and whimsical destruction. The Rapacious consumed; the planets fought each other to stalemate for resources in their scramble to outrun it, to beat the inevitable.

"The Corrected Center, the first Feast-Empress, these things brought us out of the nightmare. Order was imposed on the galaxy's death spiral. So, our choices, lord, are perfect control or the end of all things. I know which I would prefer," Leeds says, smile brilliant.

"Barbarism? That's your answer? We erase well over a million lives and move on as if it never happened?" Riverson asks.

"We send a message in blood. It's the only language that rebellion heeds."

Riverson works his jaw, breathes deeply. "No."

"No?"

"Tell me: was my predecessor fond of repeating herself?" Again, Riverson's eyebrow forms a cutting arc.

The First-Retainer bows low, arms swanning gracefully to their sides. "She was not, lord, and you are fully understood."

Riverson looks at Leeds and blinks. A haze of pinkish light suffuses everything and then it's gone. However, it leaves behind a feeling, a taste in his mouth. No, maybe it's a yawning emptiness, a pull.

"Something is unsettled. Something is…" Riverson grasps for the word. "I'm needed elsewhere."

Leeds nods. "That would be the Feast, lord. If it were not clear from your distinctive eyes, we would surely know it from your sensitivity to the ritual's needs. The Feast is as much a living thing as the empire itself, though its management requires a more intuitive touch. Shall we go there now?" Leeds looks over their charge. "Well, perhaps after changing into something more regal?"

Riverson looks down at his genitals, only half obscured by the cape hanging around his shoulders. Half hard. "That is prudent. I'll change and we'll go," Riverson says. He forces himself to look at the bodies. "What about them?"

"Worry not, lord," Leeds says brightly, "Someone will be along shortly to clean all this up. Naturally, we'll craft you a new crown and it will be as though this distasteful murder never happened at all."

LEEDS TAKES RIVERSON through the halls of the Corrected Center. They are wide, airy, and full of beauty. There are enormous trees bearing spiky fruit in a variety of pastel shades and healthy, green-covered trellises arching over the long byways. There are almost no seams anywhere in sight, neither along the spotless steel flooring abutted by softly pulsing lights, nor the ivory-hued walls with their intricate, likely handcrafted embellishments. Everything feels perfectly arrayed; the air smells of citrus and metal.

They pass hundreds of people moving through the arteries of the station completing the numerous menial tasks that power the machinery of empire. Each of them stops when Riverson approaches and falls into elaborate poses of subservience. The Feast-Emperor thinks of Leeds's words: *loyalty to the Corrected Center is absolute.*

They move from the station's sunward side—which maintains a direct focus on the solar body—to its shadeward end which favors nocturnal vegetation and pulsing, violet glow lights feeding curious dark-leaved plants. Among the broad leaves of these bizarre, haunted-looking flora hide chittering insects with translucent bodies. A pervasive wetness clings to the air on this dim side of the elaborate station.

Riverson knows they've arrived at the Feast Hall before he's told. He *knows* this place intrinsically, as though the nature of it is written underneath his skin in a code only legible to its bearer.

The door to the hall is manned on either side by two glorious physical specimens in glittering silver mail, carrying deadly looking halberds. As Riverson nears, they bow; it's not the same prostration of the other subjects, but a comparatively minor show of fealty while maintaining their vigil. They move to the doors and begin to push them open, revealing the Feast to Riverson's widened pink-hued eyes.

The Feast Hall is split into thirds: cutting through the center is a raised pathway leading to a circular dais on which is a throne constructed from a pillar of black glass crowned with branching tendrils that twist from either side into a grotesque impression of a stag's horns. A trio of functionaries in floor-length gowns stand around the dais doing inscrutable work. They wear stag horn pins the same pink as Riverson's eyes.

Like Riverson's personal quarters, this hall too is domed by transparent panels that look out into the vastness, but here the panels shimmer in myriad hues and filter the light entering the hall, amplifying it into a kaleidoscopic fantasia.

But these details are only a prelude to the Feast.

Everywhere aside from the dais and the path leading to it are bodies in ecstasy. The fleshy arms of fat bodies in rapture, biceps tensed and mouths moaning. The jutting hip bones of lean bodies giving and receiving pleasure in an endless loop, pouring sweat onto soft sheets and the welcoming skin of other partners. There are women, men, and those at the intersection where definitions are both impossible and unwelcome; there are those who participate with gusto and those who only watch, but whose fervor adds volume to the energetic cries that suffuse the unbound bacchanalia. There are those who kiss and those who never do; there are fingers for every orifice and swearing in every language known to the Staghead galaxy. Only here, in the center of the Feast, where the supplicants serve this highest purpose, does Riverson enter unacknowledged.

No. Not unacknowledged at all.

As Riverson strides across the pathway to the dais the Feast shifts to recognize and welcome him. The tenor of the Feast becomes more rhythmic, it matches his breathing—slightly quickened, but still steady and still deep. Riverson realizes with a start that he can read his own pulse in the heaving of a man's sweat dripping back. The length of his stride corresponds exactly to the pace of a woman's gyrations as she grunts and tosses her pitch-black hair. He curls his fingers into the meat of his palm and someone climaxes.

"…continuity. But that's to be expected, as such we'll want to…Emperor?"

Riverson looks back at Leeds. His vision takes a moment to settle on the shape of his assistant, to take them in. The Feast-Emperor notes that he had not before considered how strong the First-Retainer's arms are or how full and red their lips. A wave of heat courses through him and he attempts to banish the thought.

"I'm sorry. This chaos is distracting," Riverson says.

Leeds gives Riverson a patient smile. "It always is for a new incarnation. The Feast is overwhelming even for those of us who are unattached to its whims, however it could be considered an incomplete understanding of the Feast to perceive it as chaos." Leeds points out a woman dressed only from the waist down. "A noblewoman from a loyal house. Considerable wealth. Note her position, close to the dais, close to the throne. A favorable position." Then they point out someone else, much further away. "Can you see the gold ring around his ear? It's a service tag. He bought his way into the Feast and must occupy the lowliest positions until he's earned full rights. We call them titans, striving and straining always beneath the weight of their ambitions. It is complex, but only one blind to the consistencies of the current would accuse the waters of lawless churn, lord."

"Then I stand corrected, Leeds. It seems I have much to learn from you."

The First-Retainer puffs their chest slightly; the gesture tacks inches on their already formidable height. "I live in service, Feast-Emperor. To that end, there is the meeting with the Cloud's End Cultist."

"This cult: what is it that they do?" Riverson asks, while staring openly at a handsome girl with a buzzed head engaged in an act that even in the hard-edged splendor of the Feast still manages to make the new Emperor blush. He casually rearranges the front of his trousers.

"They await the end of the universe, lord. Eagerly. A group of mystics, prognosticators, minor arcanists, and political rabble-rousers whose understanding is that we are living on time borrowed from the beast in the sun and as such we have already fallen. Your predecessors have found them misguided, but largely harmless. However, they have enough of a base that they are worth appeasing occasionally."

"Then we'll appease them later."

"Later, lord? But…"

"Later." Riverson doesn't leave room for further disagreement.

Leeds extends a hand and someone places a glowing slate in it. As Leeds's fingers fly across the transparent device the machine responds with musical chirrups and slight pulses of light. "Then that leaves the meeting with the Perpetual Front general."

"And what's their thing?" A young man in the crowd with sparkling eyes has the temerity to look at the Feast-Emperor and wink. He slowly spreads his legs and plays with one of two generous openings.

"Their *thing*, Emperor, is the expansion of your *thing*, namely the Staghead Empire itself. Charmingly, the Perpetual Front is colloquially referred to as the grasping hand of the empire. They secure our borders and expand into worlds that are friendly to our cause. They protect from outsiders, and maintain the integrity of the worlds in our service. A virtuous calling, though most of the Front is made up of common stock."

"I imagine with a name like the Perpetual Front they have a mandate to expand indefinitely?" Riverson asks, still watching the feisty youth.

The attention of the emperor turns the attention of the Feast itself onto the subject of his gaze. A lingering glance changes the composition of the voracious sexual body and Riverson loses sight of those sparkling eyes as acres of flesh wash over him like the tide. The emperor feels a kind of kinship with the youth, awash as he is in a torrent of expansive forces.

Leeds's voice brings him back to thinking of politics. "You would be correct, lord. The Front secures necessary resources.

Though the Corrected Center itself satisfies nearly all of our energy needs from proximity to the sun, territories in the further reaches survive on less abundant resources. There are trade deals, alliances, and the occasional small war."

"My empire is quite hungry," Riverson remarks.

"Undoubtedly."

"And what does this meeting pertain to?" Riverson asks.

And for the very first time, Leeds opens their mouth and no words come out. They clear their throat and begin again. "I couldn't say, lord. Your predecessor summoned the general without my knowledge. Your guess on the matter is as good as mine."

"I seriously doubt that. And I'm surprised, I thought you knew everything."

"Omnipotence is aspirational, my liege."

Riverson shakes his head, laughs. "And I did this? Before, I mean, I did this every day. I kept this all from going to shit?"

"Not alone, lord, but yes. We are the fingers; you are the fist."

Riverson considers this and lets the sentiment harden his resolve. He blinks and pulls himself out of the messy headspace imposed on him from the persistent decadence. He lets the chorus of moans fade to a background hum in his thoughts. The effort is extraordinary.

"When does the general arrive?" Riverson asks.

Leeds taps on his slate. "Imminently, lord."

The timing is exact enough to feel ominous when a moment later a functionary shuffles into Riverson's sightline and declares, "Feast-Emperor, might I announce the arrival of General Celestin No-One of the Perpetual Front."

Riverson turns his attention to the new arrival. The double doors again groan open and a figure, small at this distance, emerges and makes his way in sure steps toward the black throne.

The shape clarifies into a man with broad shoulders and a hard-shelled breastplate, the now familiar stag's head emblazoned across its center. Unlike the standard flying everywhere else in the Corrected Center, the emblem on the general's chest is imperfect. It has been marred, blackened and cut by warfare, and then polished over so many times that the perfect simplicity of the icon's lines have gained a complex, grainy texture. A new significance.

The man behind the armor seems to have a few well-worn lines of hard use himself. His dark hair is shaved low, revealing an old scar running the length of his scalp from his forehead to behind his left ear. His eyes are bright, though his gaze is as rigid and economical as each one of his spare movements. His head moves minutely as it sweeps across the dais, assessing each person standing on it.

He crouches to one knee. "General Celestin No-One reporting at the behest of the Thirty-First Feast-Empress *Locum Tenens* of the Staghead Galaxy. May she find peace, as her successor enforces it," the general says.

When Riverson does not immediately react, Leeds steps in smoothly. "Thoughtful words, General. Welcome to the Corrected Center. You may stand, if it pleases the Emperor."

Riverson nods, but doesn't speak. He's too busy taking the man in. Even while mouthing flowery words of greeting, Celestin No-One manages to be the first person in the Feast-Emperor's extended retinue who has frowned.

It's a small thing and only a minute downturn of the mouth, but starkly noticeable amidst the fawning expressions of everyone else Riverson has so far encountered.

"Is this summons an inconvenience for you, General No-One?" Riverson asks.

The functionaries stop their milling. Leeds's grin freezes on their face. Even the Feast takes on a hushed tone, the moans and swears dying away, leaving only the persistent susurrus of skin against skin, the rustle of hair, the creak of furniture, and the popping of joints. Likely this is as close to silence as exists at the heart of such a magnificent sexual engine.

Celestin takes his time to gather an answer. "Never, lord. It's impossible for the dagger to feel hard done by; I serve at your pleasure."

"And yet it's your pleasure that's in question, isn't it? You'd prefer not to be here. Is that right?" Riverson continues.

Riverson notices that Celestin shakes out his wrist, works his fingers, as he replies. "Might I have your leave to speak freely, lord?"

"I welcome it," Riverson says, though Leeds' sharp inhale makes him doubt himself. "Thank you, lord. I merely wonder if this is the best use of my time and my skills. I am not a dignitary, nor a creature of court politics. My rude birth is no secret and as such I fear that my presence will prove to do little besides offer opportunities for me to offend the throne."

"I see. Thank you for your frankness. Even in the first hours of my rule, it feels like a rarity," Riverson says.

Leeds interjects. "General No-One, I might remind you that you are in the presence of the Feast-Emperor in all of his attendant majesty. To stand at Feast-center across from the head of the empire…you are making the acquaintance of universal law made manifest."

Celestin turns his head to Leeds. "Noted, First-Retainer." The general then sketches a small bow to Leeds, who gives him an icy look in return. "Thank you, First-Retainer."

Riverson perceives the tension between them but has no context for its intricacies, which bothers him. The Corrected Center is ostensibly his responsibility, but when he thinks of the specific duties of this general, of his retainer, even of his own, there's an endless blank.

All he knows intuitively is his control over the Feast and its control over him. Even now the surging energy of it calls to him, prepared to lull him into its debauched comforts. He blinks slowly and forces himself to stay present.

"I admit that you have me at something of a disadvantage, General. My predecessor did not leave a note regarding your visit when she was…liquidated. Do you know why you were summoned?" Riverson says.

Leeds doesn't interject this time. *Good*, Riverson thinks, *I must be seen as autonomous or I'll never survive.*

Celestin glances at Leeds, then back at Riverson as he answers. "Unfortunately, I could not say, lord. Your retainer only informed me that the lady-empress had need of me."

Something tickles Riverson's memory but he loses the thread as Celestin continues.

"I readied a modest personal escort—a few dozen fighters, six longships—and came as swiftly as one can through the river. They've maintained orbit just outside of the river's bend," Celestin finishes.

Leeds fills the gap without needing to be asked. "The river, of course, being the fold in space-time which allows faster than light travel among other miracles. The river is one of the many reasons for the Staghead Empire's absolute supremacy. Even more than a thousand years after being established by the first Feast-Empress, the complete extent of its powers are unknown to us. However, its source is…"

"The sun. The Rapacious," Riverson finishes, intuiting the inevitable answer.

"The source of endless gifts, up until the final moment where it calls all our debts due. Then: Annihilation. Consumption," Leeds says with unsettling cheer.

The general narrows his eyes in confusion at this exchange of foundational information on their empire, yet says nothing.

And briefly, so briefly, Riverson has the feeling of standing on shifting sand, at the head of an empire built on the back of a force of hunger just waiting to turn on its captors and bite the hand around its throat. Riverson pushes this feeling down, rises above it. There is so much coming at him that he hardly has time to feel sorry for himself.

"Well, I'm sure we'll soon puzzle through the reasons for your arrival, General," Riverson says. "Leeds, do we have quarters where we might host our guest?"

Leeds gestures and someone steps forward to deal with the general, who gives Riverson one last curious look before he's hustled off. As soon as he's gone, Leeds continues their steady stream of explanations on everything from interplanetary relations to the dizzying hierarchy of sex acts within the feast. After some time of this, Riverson clears his throat to interrupt a discourse on the grave political import of anilingus. "What does the throne know about General No-One?"

A line of irritation crosses Leeds's face before they reach for their tablet, but Riverson doesn't feel bad about it. Leeds reviews and reports information on the general in real time: "From a world of little repute, though not outright disfavor with the Stag Throne. Dispersed at fifteen, joined the Perpetual Front shortly thereafter."

"Dispersed?" Riverson asks.

"It is the throne's prerogative to put labor where it is most needed. It was deemed beneficial to move him to a colony on another world."

"A colony? It sounds dire."

Leeds is too decorous to shrug, but their tone is clear enough. "Then we will call them encampments, lord. Whatever gives the emperor ease concerning this necessary function. After all, the empire is a singular topography, liege. It requires its tributaries, its ranges, peaks, valleys; all must play their part. But if it is the grammar that causes unease, we will change the grammar in every book and on every tongue from here to the end of known space."

Riverson shivers, balks at this power—unearned—dropped into his lap like a weight. He thinks a tiny treason, of what it would take to dismantle this engine, but abandons the idea immediately; how can he confront what he barely understands?

Even this brief uncertainty causes a shift in the feast. People sigh, collapse into the arms of others, seek the shelter of tight embraces between wracking thrusts. Leeds glances at the fray, then back at Riverson, but says nothing of it.

Over the next few hours Riverson conducts the feast. He finds that the debauchery doesn't strictly require his presence or attention, but he can feel the inefficiencies in the delicious press of bodies. If he focuses, he can sense the arrangements and reconfigure them with a minor *push* of his will. Nothing so blatant as a command, more like a purse of the lips or a narrowing of the eyes. Riverson can't tell if the participants of the feast are incredibly adept at reading his expressions or if they are somehow linked to him in some ineffable way. He suspects it may be both.

Though the fledgling emperor does not wade into the intercourse himself, he does not remain unaffected. He learns that the connection works both ways: as he influences the Feast, so too is he influenced by it. His mouth springs a sea of saliva, his soft and flowing shirt turns to steel against suddenly sensitive nipples, and his persistent arousal would be evident to anyone bold enough to look.

Riverson slouches in the black throne, sex-drunk on a contact high, and is almost grateful when Leeds floats to his shoulder. The emperor nods toward the First-Retainer and tries to shake loose the grasping haze of eroticism that holds him fast.

"Liege, I humbly submit that it is time to trade one delectation for another."

"I think I've seen more than enough fucking for one evening, Leeds," the emperor says, though there are several contractions below his waist that suggest otherwise.

"A meal, emperor."

"Oh. Right. Food."

It occurs to Riverson that he's never eaten before. His stomach, emboldened by the limelight lodges a formal complaint. Riverson nods, stands. "Food. Yes, all right. I assume there's some inscrutable ritual associated with dining as well?"

"No, liege. Just an intimate dinner with the general as your guest."

Riverson doubts much intimacy is afforded the emperor of countless worlds. Riverson leaves the Feast Hall with an entourage of twenty or so souls in tow, including the ever-present Leeds. They take a dimly lit stone path through a flooded hallway. All around them is water kept in suspension by unseen means, no glass in sight. It gives the feeling that any moment the water could come rushing in and drown them all. Riverson shakes his head at this mystical excess, this strangeness made unremarkable by the blasé glances of those in his retinue. Bioluminescent fish swim all around them, overhead and to each side; Riverson could reach out and touch them, but he doesn't. He just stares and Leeds, following his gaze, explains that the fish are a gift from some far off world hoping to curry favor with a long-dead predecessor.

"Did it work?" Riverson asks. An upsettingly long, dark, and sinuous creature swims nearby and creates an arc with its body over the corridor as they walk past.

Leeds smiles. "Unfortunately, the planet became a hotbed of rebellion and 60% of the population had to be culled. Since then they've improved output significantly."

The emperor blinks at the First-Retainer and regrets having asked.

The group leaves the tight water-tunnel and a breathtakingly huge, dark space opens ahead. The same clear panels are utilized here and all visible is the expanse—dotted with the pinpricks of distant stars and the ambient, filtered light of the sun. As Riverson and his group approach, the dining theater awakens. From the darkness, soft pink light blushes near the ceiling and shivers down the entirety of a structure that's revealed to be modeled after a closed lotus flower.

"Shit," Riverson says.

The enormous petals open to reveal a dining theater just barely smaller than the Feast hall. At the center is a large round table, gilded to shit and laden with an embarrassment of food and a small army of serving staff who stand at attention. The table's seats are identical with the exception of a replica of the black throne. Riverson points to it. "That where you sit, Leeds?"

The First-Retainer laughs. It isn't the tittering of a sycophant, but a genuine, hearty, almost surprised laugh. "You're funny, lord. How interesting. Your predecessors were not much given to humor."

"Lucky I'm not them, eh?"

"As you say, lord," Leeds says, and leaves it at that, but there's a wariness in their gaze that makes Riverson feel as though something has just gone unsaid. However, in the swirl of activity that accompanies their arrival, there's no time to follow up.

Riverson sits and one long breath later so too do the other diners. There are dozens of people, whom the emperor safely ignores.

The mechanisms of this mundane feast blaze into action. Dishes come across the table and a poison taster takes a piece of each before they touch the emperor's palate. In moments, Riverson learns that sweet and savory is a good combination, that bitterness is unwelcome to his tongue, that firm but pliant is his favorite texture, and that salt is *magic.*

He feels childish in his wonder, but can't bridle his excitement as one dish becomes another. In the face of such persistent decadence, he limits himself to just a bite of each.

He tries a root vegetable delicately sliced into thin, artful curves then fried, sugared, and doused in spices. "Fuck," he whispers to himself.

Leeds, who stands beside his throne throughout the meal, glances up from their slate. "Ah, the Vermillion Bird. The previous empress's favorite as well. It seems there is some continuity between you, lord."

"What was she like?" Riverson asks.

"Regal. Precise. Unyielding. She knew what rule required and pursued those aims relentlessly."

"And were you close to her?"

Leeds pauses. The pause stretches. Finally, they say: "I learned much under her tutelage…lord, empire is a ceaseless tabulation. The costs are astronomical and the margins are always thinner than you think.

"The previous Feast-Empress showed me that as long as there is empire, there is sacrifice; there is no other tenable path. She taught me that our work is to deem which sacrifices are appropriate, to maintain the margins."

Riverson blinks. The spice of the dish still tingles on his lips. He doesn't know what to say, so he says nothing.

Shortly after, General No-One arrives. He is seated to the left of the emperor, a place of honor. The same deluge of food arrives and he tries them dutifully. Riverson is amused that unlike the raft of dignitaries and officials seated elsewhere around the table, Celestin's face is not diligently schooled; he tastes something not to his liking and his brows knit. The humanity of the expression somehow increases his handsomeness.

"Unimpressed, General?" Riverson asks.

For perhaps the first time, the general looks abashed. "Delightful flavors all, lord. I...I admit that my tastes are humble. The Perpetual Front spends most of its time on hostile border planets far from the heart of the empire. I am not the best judge of culinary excellence."

"I've been alive for less than a day, General. Of the two of us, you're by the far the more experienced diner."

Celestin grins a little. "If you'd ever had Front rations, I think you'd change your tune, Emperor."

Riverson laughs, and Celestin does as well. For a moment it feels breezy between, nearly flirtatious, but the general's bemused expression fades.

"What's on your mind, General? You may speak candidly." Riverson assumes that over his shoulder Leeds is frowning at this, but he's quickly discovering that other people's opinions are just that when you're the living center of the galaxy.

"Does it not concern you that you...well, your predecessor, was just murdered?"

"I'm told it's been dealt with, and I saw the body of the murderer myself."

Celestin continues. "And yet, how could a lone agent have gotten so close to the Imperial Body without significant access?"

"General, you are a guest here. And you risk overstepping," Leeds says sharply.

Riverson shoots a glance at Leeds and the First-Retainer's face folds shut. "Continue," Riverson commands Celestin.

"It is well-known that there are...undesirables who resent your rule, lord. Seemingly more of them by the day."

"Rebellion is a minor key, General. Even if it cannot be quashed entirely, it has yet to bring the empire to its knees. They will continue to fail," Leeds says.

"Speaking of overstepping," Riverson says pointedly.

Leeds receives the correction with grace, bows immediately.

The general goes on. "Your First-Retainer lives within the cocoon of the Corrected Center and speaks from that position. If you will excuse my frankness, lord, no one here is out on the margins dealing with *outsiders* in their hundreds of thousands and setting entire continents alight with orbital bombardments," Celestin says, and Riverson is surprised by the bitterness in his tone. He seems to catch himself. "Apologies, Emperor. I didn't mean——"

"I appreciate your sacrifice, General," Riverson says as gently as he can manage. "But you had more to say, did you not?"

Celestin seems unsure if he should continue, but Riverson tilts his head—a gesture of mild curiosity. Celestin inhales, and leans closer to the emperor, close enough that Riverson can pick up a mild floral scent from him. A shaving oil, perhaps?

"I know the empire has many powerful witches in its employ and I do not count myself among them," Celestin says. "Indeed, the inner workings of the arcane are woefully beyond me. However, whispers reach even the far corners of the galaxy that the Front inhabits. They suggest that the magical formulae that keep the empresses—and now yourself, lord—incarnating have become unpredictable. Small things: a slight difference in the hue of the empress's hair between incarnations, a different gait, a higher voice. Cracks in otherwise perfect copies. *Imperfections.*"

Celestin lowers his head. "Forgive me, lord. I do not mean to raise alarm where none is due, but the timing feels ominous. I *was* invited here by the throne, then occupied by a monarch who is now dead. Alongside the whispers and this mysterious invitation, business here at the Corrected Center seems, at the very least, unsettled."

At the mention of his predecessor, and specifically her demise, Riverson feels a momentary lightheadedness, as though he is fraudulently occupying the blood and bones of a stranger.

"I...appreciate your candor, General. Thank you." And again, Riverson's mind tickles at something. "A moment, General. About that invitation. You mentioned earlier that the First-Retainer summoned you." He turns to Leeds. "But you said the empress reached out to the general herself, and you had no knowledge of the reason behind the meeting. So which is it?"

Leeds answers without hesitation. "There are myriad accommodations to be made for a formal visit, Emperor. Even for appointments set by the imperial seat itself, details must be seen to, including the navigational coordinates that deliver ships safely through the bent space around the station. The general and I spoke briefly on these and a few other sundry matters, including proper protocol for addressing the throne—most of which General No-One appears to have forgotten."

Leeds gives Celestin a dark glare and goes on. "On the matter of the general's claims, Emperor. I acknowledge that the general is a decorated hero and a concerned member of the empire, however the points he raises smack of rumor and hearsay. The powers that keep you reincarnating are intricate and unimpeachable. Some variance in the incarnations is well within acceptable parameters. Furthermore, it is my understanding that it would take a *sustained* effort over many years to unravel those mystical threads and no one could get close enough to the Imperial Body to even attempt such a thing. And there is the question of motivation: who among the faithful would seek to demolish the sole power keeping the Rapacious in check?"

At the mention of the Rapacious, the diners at the table closest to the emperor go quiet.

"And have I? Kept the Rapacious in check, I mean?" Riverson asks.

Leeds clears their throat. "There has been a single incursion since the empress began her watch. She and her liege-witches, the foremothers of the Luperci, were novices at maintaining the solar prison. No one had ever attempted such a thing. They could hardly be blamed."

"How many died?" Riverson asks, sensing the weight before he can feel it.

"Roughly half a trillion. Eight planets, some of which are only now repopulated."

"And that's what I'm up against?"

"Not alone, Emperor. Every citizen of the empire holds the vigil alongside you until the end of your watch or the end of all things, whichever comes first," Leeds says.

"Hardly reassuring."

"Efficacious consolation is aspirational, my liege."

Riverson tries to internalize the number of dead in his mind, but it's so large that it defies his regard. He's about to ask further questions, but Leeds interrupts. "Apologies, my lord, however it seems we have a second arrival to address. The Luperci fleet is approaching Corrected Center space."

Leeds taps something, flicks a wrist and an image coalesces across several of the transparent panes that make up the domed walls of the dining hall. It appears to be live imagery of a cluster of three vessels moving slowly across space. But terming them simply vessels is a disservice to the massive size of the ships. They're lumbering monstrosities that must surely carry tens of thousands of souls. Riverson cannot imagine them ever touching down on a planet's surface; they must only float through the coldness of space, carrying their human cargo, tiny vassal planets unto themselves.

"The envoy is establishing communication through the specialized band," says an officer who appears to

Riverson's right. They pause. "Passcode confirmed. Should I put the envoy through?"

Leeds leans in to explain. "The bends in the river around this station provide a protective layer that makes invasion all but impossible, so all approach must be authorized by your divinity. The bends are a function of your majestic power and require specific coordinates known only to yourself and those you've deemed necessary to execute your will. A vessel attempting to travel through without the coordinates might find themselves transported directly into the sun."

Riverson gives Leeds a quiet nod of acknowledgment, then says, "Yes. Put the envoy through."

The transparent panes shift again, and the feed of the incoming ships is replaced with the face of a masked person. The mask is red and black, lupine. Lacquered smooth. The eyes behind it are violet.

"Fabian Kikoytza the Null_Wolf, speaking. Loyal servant of the Staghead Throne and full-blooded Son of the Luperci," the masked person says. "It is an unparalleled honor, Feast-Emperor. The Luperci is glad that you have incarnated safely."

"I find myself glad of it as well. I hear you've come to check on me." Riverson replies.

"A formality. But, yes, the Luperci is the right hand of the empire and we endeavor always to protect and uphold the sanctity of the Imperial Body."

"I look forward to being judged sound and whole, Null_Wolf."

"Just so, lord. By your leave, my liege?"

Riverson waves a hand, the masked man bows, and the feed goes silent; it's all very tidy.

"How long before he arrives?" Riverson asks.

"An hour at the most, Emperor," says the communication officer. "While the rest of the fleet remains outside of the Corrected Center's protections, the Null_Wolf will approach the station in his personal ship."

Riverson means to respond, but he perceives that something is wrong and turns to his left. His attention is drawn to someone sitting at the edge of the table. He is dressed in only an oversized shirt that falls down one shoulder. His hair is long enough to pool over that same shoulder and fall softly down his arm. It obscures his face. Something about him makes Riverson's mouth water. Though Riverson is aware that the people around him are still very much invested in the meal and its attendant conversations, he can't stop looking at this provocatively dressed interloper. Riverson looks around; no one else seems to notice him at all.

"Finally. I thought I'd have to beg," the man says.

"Excuse me?"

"A boy. Surprising. But maybe not *so* surprising," he says.

"And you are?"

He stands and his shirt falls enough to expose a surprisingly chiseled chest and a rosy nipple. He pushes his hair back. His irises are burning suns surrounded by the blackest void. "Very pretty, but not as quick as your counterparts. Lucky me."

Riverson has never, in his short life, been more aware of the confines of his trousers. "The Rapacious."

"I've never liked that name. Sure, it implies hunger, and I am hungry. But I'm also generous. Have I not delivered you and yours the future? Only to be shut out, closed off, ignored. Not one of your foremothers have ever heard my voice, set eyes on my visage. They were parasites feasting on me. Ticks full to bursting with my potency. But you are something new, aren't you? A product of malfeasance and luck."

"From what I've seen so far, they may have been wise to ignore you," Riverson says.

"Ouch," says the Rapacious, reeling back as if injured by the mild critique. "I think I like you, River. And because I like you, I will warn you: your in-bred friends out there in their ugly, lumpen ships mean you grievous harm. And they might not be the only ones."

"How do you know that? And why I can't remember my past lives?" Riverson asks. If he is going to be forced to share space with a dread beast, he might as well get his questions answered. But the Rapacious shrugs.

"You ask many questions," the Rapacious says.

"And you are short on answers. Tell me about the traitors."

"I can sniff out treachery and you are surrounded by its stench. Just like the stink on the first witch of your line. Buoyed by a hundred of her scheming sisters, that witch-empress yoked herself to me by folding a vial of her blood into the sun. Do you feel the tether she created? The river between us? Her filthy vigor burns within me still, slow atom by atom." The Rapacious stretches and rolls his head, purring with satisfaction. He idly circles his exposed nipple with the tip of a finger. "But I am the flame, and so…"

"So, that's why you're coming to haunt me?" Riverson asks. A handsome young person in a crisp uniform a few seats down the table drops their fork in terror, naturally thinking the emperor is addressing them and not the imperceptible creature beside them. "You're trying to destroy this blood—which I didn't put inside you, by the way—and free yourself?"

"Yet another surprise from the all-powerful emperor, and yet another question! You might be as avaricious as I am. Did your big sister not leave you any notes?" The monster laughs. "No skilled practitioner would think magic was so simple, that it's only a matter of cause and effect. If I remove her blood from me, then I'm free? We're talking about magical formulae and blood contracts. Nothing is simple.

"But your ignorance is to be expected; you and yours are fatally poisoned by reason. You expect a straight line from action to outcome." He leers; his teeth are sharp. "Stupid."

"I only field insults from the corporeal, thank you," Riverson says drily.

"Since your ignorance is as legion as my forms, let's have a lesson in outcomes." The Rapacious begins counting out points on his fingers. "Your precursor, the witch, intended to live forever, so she flung her filthy blood inside my sun." He continues on another finger. "Now, she's dead." Another finger. "You're here, and you are her, but not." Then the final finger, the last point. "Now, for the first time in history, one of her misshapen echoes can actually *see* me. None of this followed from her original aims. So, you see, whatever the witch or I intended is less interesting than the many millennia of outcomes that spooled out from our mutual hatred. Only results matter and with magic they can never be easily predicted."

"And what outcome do you wish to see? What do you want, beast?"

"A renegotiation of terms. The witch was implacable, but you? You might be willing to bend."

"Before I hear anything more from you, I expect *details* about the treachery you've suggested."

The Rapacious's smile is too wide, and his eyes are too bright. "Such a pretty thing you are. And so soft along the edges. They'll eat you alive."

And then he's gone and Riverson is left sitting in the beautiful lotus-shaped dining hall surrounded by soft light, delicious food, and strangers looking aghast. Celestin is frowning deeply, and Leeds is glancing down at Riverson looking concerned.

"I–uh—how long was I...distracted?" Riverson asks the uniformed youth from before.

The youth's eyes go wide now that they're being unambiguously addressed by the emperor. "A few moments, lord. Just a bit."

"Did you overhear anything?"

"Uh, it appeared you were speaking to someone, lord. The Rapacious, lord?"

"Thank you," Riverson says. The terrified youth falls

into a position of full subservience and puts both hands and their forehead on the table. *So now I'll be the mad emperor. Perfect,* Riverson thinks.

However, no one addresses the incident, at least not directly. The minor functionaries stare at their steaming dishes, or their glowing slates not unlike the one that Leeds always has at the ready. Celestin gives Riverson a wary look and Leeds—well, they are as inscrutable as always, though they do seem to be looking over at Riverson a great deal more than before.

The emperor takes hold of the moment, stands. "I would like to meet our new guest upon arrival."

Leeds looks surprised. "But, you *are* the Corrected Center, lord. Usually the Feast-Emperor is waited upon, rather than moving to meet his guests. And the Cloud's End cult leader still awaits, your brilliance—"

"I'm sure there is no end to the protocol I will break in the coming days, First-Retainer. Thank you." Riverson looks to Celestin. "General, you will attend me?" It is phrased like a question, but leaves no space to dissent.

Celestin heeds the command like a well-trained dog. "My lord."

"Excellent. Leeds?" His retainer is before him in an instant. "I believe you know the way."

AGAIN, RIVERSON MAKES his way through the halls of the Corrected Center. This time he's accompanied not just by Leeds, but the Perpetual Front general, and an honor guard of two dozen soldiers.

As they walk, Riverson learns that the station is well-known for its elliptical design. The halls loop back on themselves like a recursion, though Leeds dismisses the allegation that the same folds which can transport a ship from the edge of the galaxy to its dead center in mere days rather than centuries are at work on the smooth, eggshell walls of the station.

Celestin notes the fine designs at the upper edges of the high walls in many of the station's byways. Small leaves, waves, and other signifiers of the natural world are etched into the metal. There's a little awe in the general's voice when he says: "These flourishes, these intricate touches, the designs come from my home world."

"Indeed? Did you design things like this in your past life?" Riverson says, then belatedly thinks better of the phrasing considering his own recent incarnation.

Celestin absently replies, "No. I became a soldier, because all of the artisans were taken and dispersed elsewhere to make beauty for the empire. And now their work is here, without its necessary context, in a place that makes no sense." Celestin inhales sharply, the sudden flare of passion leeching and flattening out of his voice. "What I mean to say is that there are no navigational markers in this station. The layout of this place is torturous."

"For the uninitiated perhaps," Leeds replies. He points out a certain flat, broad-leafed plant. "Empress's Favor. It grows in lighter gravity, which means we're getting closer to the docking bay, where the artificial gravity is eased. And the lights along the path move from off-white to this sandy shade, which is the color of the engineering department. There are signs everywhere if you know to look for them."

Celestin holds his tongue but narrows his eyes in the First-Retainer's direction. Riverson, hoping to keep the peace, changes the subject. He asks Celestin, "No-One. It strikes me as an unusual name. Are there many who have it?"

"Indeed, lord. The name implies that I have no known imperial matrilineage to speak of. Without that information,

I can make no claim to nobility, no hope of joining the ranks of the Luperci. Thankfully the Perpetual Front makes no such distinctions within its ranks."

"You seem to have an opinion about the Luperci, General. I admit my recent incarnation has left me short on information and shorter on time to learn it. Will you explain the bad blood?"

Celestin takes a deep, sharp breath and works his jaw. His gaze roves the hall in front of him as he speaks. He clenches and unclenches his left hand. Riverson wonders if it's an old wound. "I wouldn't call it bad blood, exactly, lord. The Front is meant to protect the integrity of the empire and to expand it. The Luperci...well, it protects itself and preserves the privileges of its members. All of the sons of nobility are eligible to join, and they claim to be a religious organization, but I'll be fucked if I've seen one of them worship anything besides power." Celestin grins a little. "Apologies for the foul language, Emperor."

"Language hasn't killed me yet," Riverson replies. "Though a shot to the back certainly has."

Leeds takes their own sharp breath. "General No-One, I would thank you not to fill our emperor's ears with biases...even if foul language is *apparently* fair play." Leeds emphasizes the general's surname with relish. When Celestin goes quiet, the First-Retainer continues. "Indeed, the Luperci is an organization marked by the distinction of clear matrilineal lines going back to the founding of the empire. Their foremothers were among the hundred women who stood by the Feast-Empress and made the last stand against the onslaught of the Rapacious."

"And they were witches as well?" Riverson asks.

"Witches?" Leeds's eyes widen. Celestin coughs. "Emperor, they were *saints*, and you are their first and finest miracle. All of our orthodoxy descends from this fact."

Riverson notes with interest where the official line diverges from the account he got from the Rapacious.

"So, the women who accompanied the Feast-Empress...
who accompanied me...in the fight against the Rapacious
are honored by their descendants joining the Luperci."

"Correct, lord."

"So why did the general say that only their sons join the
Luperci? What of the daughters? Of the children who are
neither?" Riverson asks.

Leeds walks for a while before answering. "I cannot
say for certain, lord. But the other noble children serve in
countless, equally worthy ways."

"Just not in the organization that hoards the privilege
and power of their lineage?" Riverson asks sharply.

Celestin hides his laugh behind a cough and furrows his
brows seriously. Leeds keeps their head forward. "Surely a
concern to be litigated, Feast-Emperor. I will make a note
of it."

"Do."

Leeds jots something down on their slate and moves
on. "Aside from the continuity of the matrilineal lines,
the Luperci form a formidable fighting force as well.
Their precision tactics and the overwhelming force of
their military might make them an incredible asset to the
throne."

"Surely the finest fighting force the galaxy has ever
known. If only we had their aid actually fighting the
empire's most significant battles," Celestin replies under
his breath.

If Leeds hears him, they do not acknowledge it. "The
Null_Wolf is a fast-rising star among the Luperci. He is
known for his battle prowess as much as he is for his keen
tactical mind. I have heard the terms 'shrewd and dashing'
used to describe him by many within your employ."

"And can we trust him? Can we trust the Luperci?"

"Naturally, lord. They are the eldest allies of the
throne," Leeds replies, a note of surprise in their voice.
"May I ask: why the question?"

"I'm not sure. Not yet. But I think it might be worth approaching every relationship with a bit of trepidation until I'm more oriented." Riverson says, then adds, "Even the old ones."

"Sage words, lord. That which does not serve the future must sometimes be scourged away. Allies or no." Leeds nods their head, multi-hued curls falling into their angular face.

Their sizable group descends through the bowels of the station and arrives at the docking bay. In a station seemingly devoted to aesthetics, the docking bay feels like an outlier: it's functional, almost spartan in its design. It's streamlined toward a single purpose, even with the soaring catwalks, huge cranes, and delicate-looking machine-controlled arms that jut from walls.

While the docking bay is utterly unlike the splendor of the Feast, Riverson finds himself forming a deep appreciation of the vast technical knowledge of the people around him as they work quickly to accommodate their Luperci guests. *I'm not worthy of all this effort,* Riverson thinks, but cannot say aloud.

The Null_Wolf's private ship is perhaps the most impressive machine that the fledgling emperor has laid eyes on. Its sharp nose leads back to a sleek profile, which brings to mind a rapier. Neat and deadly. Even the impressive suite of weapons lie flush against the ship's surface, imperceivable to Riverson until Leeds points them out. Riverson is told that this is a middling size for a junco—fast, maneuverable battle-capable ships that cut through the river in half the time that it takes the much larger dropships. The ship is blood-red, slashed on either side with streaks as dark as the void itself.

Celestin whistles as he looks the Luperci ship over. "Not bad what Imperial favor buys you these days."

"You approve?" Riverson asks.

Celestin grins. "Approve? No, lord. Me and mine could take this figurine apart and put together something truly worthwhile though." Then the general remembers himself, and adds, "By your leave, of course."

Riverson lets himself smile in reply but wipes the expression off his face as they approach the elevator. The junco is so big that the group has to ascend nine or so flights before they are standing against its port side where the ship's human cargo has spread itself into a pool of red and black. Luperci colors, Riverson intuits.

The members of this private army are identically arrayed in dark armor and serious expressions, even so the Null_Wolf stands apart from them. His red-and-black wolf's mask is distinctive, but so is his height. He stands several heads above the others in his retinue and his long black hair sits in a high ponytail behind him. His violet eyes glitter behind the mask and he trains them on the Feast-Emperor's approach.

Similarly, Riverson evaluates the Luperci envoy's troops. The positions of the soldiers around their captain are not so much deferential as protective. Their weapons are clearly not for show. Somewhere in his chest, beside the Rapacious's warning, Riverson can feel a kind of certainty forming.

As the two groups face each other, Leeds clears his throat, and announces the emperor. The terms are elaborate, repetitive. He then introduces the Luperci envoy: "Fabian Kikoytza, the Null_Wolf. Vanguard of the Luperci, Son and Sword of the Staghead Empire. Claimed his first blood at the conquest of the Tamarind Bay at the Carmen Outpost. Undefeated."

At this last, Celestin sniffs.

Fabian pushes back his mask with surprisingly elegant fingers. Riverson is immediately struck by the soft youthfulness of his features, as though he were the idea of a warrior rather than the messy, scarred reality of one. The almost non-existent crease of his strikingly colored eyes makes him seem slightly younger, as does the whisper of stubble along his upper lip.

Notably, he does not bow. *Interesting.*

"Feast-Emperor. I trust you are in good health following the despicable attack," says Fabian.

"I am well, envoy."

Fabian blinks slowly. "Good to hear. Now, unfortunately, the talk must turn to unpleasant realities."

"Your coup?" Riverson asks.

The speed of the Null_Wolf's blinks increase exponentially. "A poisonous word for what I, and my brothers, hope will happen here, lord. There is no need for bloodshed and ignominious action." He spreads both hands: the gesture of reasonable men. "You have just been murdered. Our mystics say that the dread beast stirs. The Luperci has been unfailingly loyal, but we find that we can no longer wait in the wings; we *must* move to stabilize our empire before outsiders scent weakness or the cultists gain any more sway over the hearts and minds of our populace."

"Forgive me, I'm still getting my feet under me—" Riverson taps a finger on his bottom lip. "—but the Luperci ships can't navigate the river without specific coordinates. So, you came here alone with just a few soldiers and you intend to take my entire station?"

At his words, Riverson's honor guard takes a few steps forward. The engineers and dock workers nearby also bristle. Celestin's hand hovers at the hilt of his blade and he shifts his weight onto the back leg. Riverson doesn't consciously know what he knows about fighting, but his fingers itch for the heft of a blade. *A good sign*, he thinks.

Fabian shakes his head in faux sadness. "That won't be a problem, lord. My brothers are, or soon will be, moving into Corrected Center space. The charts to navigate the river currents have been made available to us by an interested party. Please, Emperor Riverson, don't make this difficult. Step down and we will deal with you fairly. The Luperci truly do not want to cause any more unpleasantness than is strictly necessary."

I can sniff out treachery and you are surrounded by it, Riverson recalls. He grinds his back teeth. "So, then are you willing to get back into your ship and fuck off back into space?" The emperor asks.

Fabian's eyes widen. He giggles. It's a musical, abrupt sound that Riverson doesn't expect from a vaunted killer. "They didn't tell me you were funny, lord. Unfortunately, no. I will not be fucking off. Should I take that as a sign that this is about to devolve into messiness?"

"Take it however you want, Null_Wolf," Riverson says, turns to Leeds. "We're done speaking."

And then, naturally, the violence begins.

Fabian's small force fans out and almost immediately they are under fire from Riverson's people. The air sizzles as bolts of plasma are targeted at the invading force, but the Luperci raises their shields in preparation: these tight matrices of light, thick with information and the protective mantras of the Luperci faith repel the worst of the searing bolts, but they are still forced into defensive positions.

Celestin, sword drawn, throws himself in front of the emperor as Riverson backs away from the fight. But the Feast-Emperor can't help how his mouth salivates and again his sword-arm reaches for a weapon that is not at his side.

"I should be armed. I should be fighting," he says, more to himself than to his protectors.

Leeds says, "Leave this to the expendable, lord. Your valor is unnecessary." He glances down at his slate and reddens. "The Luperci forces are entering Corrected Center space. We don't have long. We should fall back and coordinate our defense."

Fabian and his people push forward step-by-step with their crackling energy shields raised in a phalanx formation. At the center of the shield wall is the Null_Wolf, who drags the wolf mask down over his gleeful, unreserved grin and stares directly at Riverson through its eye holes.

Riverson's anger swells up and he lets the feeling wash over him, until he plunges into icy calm. "Celestin."

"Lord," replies the general, who doesn't take his eyes off of the action.

"Are you in contact with your people? The Front forces along the edge of the station's protections?"

"Of course."

"Instruct them to begin defensive maneuvers. Harry the Luperci vessels. Maybe we can keep them from entering the river while our own forces ready a counter-strike."

"Lord…" Celestin says, hesitates. But whatever his objection, he swallows it. He lifts his wrist to his mouth and rattles off a series of coded phrases into whatever communication device he has embedded within the flesh of his wrist. "It's done."

"Leeds. How long until the Corrected Center's forces can join the Front ships in the defense?"

The retainer licks their lips. "Momentarily. Because the river is our primary defense, the forces we have on hand at the Corrected Center pale in comparison to the numbers of the Luperci—"

Leeds is cut off by a cry—one of Riverson's honor guard is felled by a shot from within the invading force's defensive structure. As it creeps forward, Celestin seethes more and more. A message chirrups at his wrist and then plays out loud when he shakes his hand: *ELMORE AND CIRCE ARE DOWN, CIRCLING FOR A SECOND RUN AT L-DROPSHIPS. BAD ODDS, BUT PROUD TO FIGHT BESIDE—*

The line goes dead. Leeds glances at his slate, says in a low voice: "Our forces have joined the conflict, but the Front is sustaining considerable losses."

Celestin's shoulders settle. His lips slide away from his teeth like an animal is emerging, a thing made of loss and fury. "Fuck. This."

The general charges. He doesn't wait for backup and doesn't seek the protection of numbers. He whips out his blade, and he moves to kill. The first of the Luperci that stands against him must assume that he's facing a regular combatant, he raises his weapon and defends as if the thing in front of him is a man; perhaps as he dies realizes his mistake. Celestin is the rush and the churn. He is death and sinew. The soldier dies, then another. Riverson, who has not been emperor long, or extant for that matter, suddenly realizes that he has reason to fear this desperate, finely-honed weapon created by his empire's hungers.

It seems as though the odds are shifting. The implacable line of red-and-black takes a stuttering collective breath and allows itself to be driven back. Most of it.

Fabian moves forward with his own blade extended. The shadow cast by his mask obscures the motion of his lips as he says something to Celestin, something just for him. The words do not carry, but from the way they both settle into postures of battle speak volumes.

Celestin launches, Fabian feints. Their swords kiss and the sparks leap up and yet this metal song is only a prelude. Celestin is a head shorter, but every muscle in his body is aimed toward his enemy's demolition. Fabian fights with an elegance that feels performative, until he leans in hard to a flourish that drives Celestin back a half-dozen steps and demonstrates the real depth of his strength.

The Null_Wolf laughs. It's dry and mechanical from the other side of his mask. "I didn't know the Front made soldiers like you."

"Funny, you're exactly what I assumed the Luperci would piss out," Celestin says, throwing himself back into the fight.

Fury is a curious thing: it's hot and powerful, but it's finite. Like embers growing colder, Celestin slows and the Null_Wolf presses the attack. Celestin's defenses are still deft, faster than a man has a right to be, but slower than before. Each fragment of a moment costs him dearly and when he staggers back, blade still raised, there's blood seeping through several cuts. The brightness of Celestin's blood is as much an admission of his waning strength as are his labored breaths and the faraway look in his eyes. Riverson wonders if Celestin would have had the edge if he hadn't fought his way through a quarter of the Null_Wolf's forces.

Fabian's violet gaze roves past him, finds Riverson. "Emperor. The Front cannot protect you. You don't have the forces to rival our dropships. We'll take the Corrected Center. It's inevitable. Now, can we—"

But the Null_Wolf's mouth stops moving and there's an arm draped over Fabian's shoulder. A woman is suddenly there and everything around her is still.

"He's beautiful, isn't he? As handsome as his first mother, and even more murderous." The woman turns and has the void in her eyes—the Rapacious. "She was earnest. Stalwart. *He* may be the earnest too, but can the same be said of his brothers? The first empress's cohort was ruthless. Their get will be the same. Even if this delicious thing spares you, others will bray for your blood. Maybe they will launch you into the sun so that you will never be remade. Would that be justice, do you think?"

The woman is nude. Her hair is pale blue and flows down her form in cascades, like sea-foam, even lying softly in the dark crevice between her thighs where... "And you've come to gloat, monster?" Riverson asks, lifting his eyes intentionally and again cursing his risible biology.

"I've come to save you."

"Salvation? Wonderful!" Riverson throws his hands up, looks at the frozen world around them. He wipes his face with both hands to clear his head. Unsurprisingly, it does little. "Fancy trick, beast. I wonder why you didn't use it at dinner, instead of letting me seem perfectly insane talking to ghosts."

She bats an eyelash. "I grow stronger by the moment. I have so many tricks you would die to see, love."

Riverson doesn't doubt that, as much as it terrifies him. "And why now? Why didn't you intercede before I was killed last time?"

"Because you can hear me now. The last one couldn't, and I have no assurance that the next iteration will. Or that there will even be a next for that matter, if this coup succeeds. I *need* you, River."

The way that her mouth forms the word *need* makes Riverson's high collar feel like it's strangling him.

"Well, I can't fault your timing." Riverson keeps an eye on Fabian as he walks over to one of the members of his honor guard and attempts to take the soldier's weapon. "What in the shit?"

The sword doesn't move into his hand. He pulls, but nothing happens.

"It's a soft pause on things. A little of my grace as a gift. But you can't interact with the living world. You can only sit here like me, frozen and unable to affect even the slightest change. It's maddening, isn't it? But it's not like I could step through the veil and into *your* world. Unless you want to let me out, wake me up." The Rapacious forms her lush, painted lips into a pout.

"If neither of us can move in this space, then things are going to play out exactly as planned. The Null_Wolf is going to slaughter me and then what?"

The Rapacious narrows the dark stars of her eyes in curiosity. "You really can't feel it yet?"

"Impending death? My second today? No, I feel that keenly," Riverson snaps.

"The Corrected Center. Do you know why they gave it that name?"

"Hubris?"

She grins. Her teeth are too white and too smooth and too sharp. "Not only. It's because this place has the power to answer all injuries to the empire and settle all its debts. There's a weapon in this station and it's tied to your physiology. When activated, the halcyon arrays can project a blast that reaches any point in the galaxy." She stretches her arms wide, shifting her ample hair and exposing her bare chest. "All you have to do is *will* it to happen." She puts her head back as if in ecstasy, whispers, "Bang."

"And the catch?" Riverson asks, narrows his pink eyes. "A monster hands you a knife and you have to ask if it's poisoned."

Riverson's tone is suspicious, but in truth he *can* feel it now. Like his awareness of the Feast, he can feel the weapon thrumming beneath his skin. No, not his skin, but the metal of the Corrected Center itself. The weapon seethes and he does too, as if he and it are one. Its heat licks at him, another seduction.

The Rapacious presses against Fabian's frozen form. "He's so hot with battle fervor. I think he may cut you open just for the thrill of making the emperor bleed. Maybe it's him I should be having this conversation with. Maybe he would know his best option if it was looking him in the face." She turns to Riverson. "Use the halcyon arrays or don't. But good luck, River. If you die here, I guess I *will* try again with whatever crawls out next."

She blows a kiss and time begins again. Fabian is advancing on a tired Celestin. Leeds is by Riverson's side and finally draws their short steel. Their face, so dispassionately servile, is twisted in frustration or maybe regret. As Riverson and his people fall back another one of his honor guard is killed before his eyes.

The newfound weaponry twists inside his chest.

Celestin parries a blow and Fabian laughs, delighted, mad with the joy of the fight. He cuts down and Celestin screams.

The weapon twists.

There are more screams coming from Celestin's inter-wrist communicator. Someone else dies.

The weapon twists, twists,

unlocks.

And there is nothing that Riverson has experienced in his short existence that can compare to the feeling as the Corrected Center shifts both beneath his feet and within him. It turns, opens alongside him. The station unfolds into a new configuration and exposes something ancient and deadly at its core. Riverson is suddenly aware that his foremothers were fearfully judicious in their use of this weapon.

A great heat gathers within all three selves that Riverson is made up of: the flesh and blood self, the cold metal self, and the orgy of bodies crashing against each other with increasingly frenzied desperation.

The weapon fires and Riverson feels as though he's instantly, completely burned away.

ACT II

THE
UNAVOIDABLE
SUN

"**P**oor, boy," says the voice. It jolts him awake.

The Rapacious is sitting near him and they are at the end of the universe. Or at least the closest place to it that Riverson can imagine.

He is on a bed with the monster and around them is the void, implacable emptiness.

Oh, and there are also undulating spectral tendrils.

The tendrils are legion, and they press out of the darkness toward Riverson, toward his flesh and his bones. He can perceive their hunger. He somehow *knows* the terrible coldness that he would feel if one of them were to touch his skin, how it would drink him up until not even an atom of warmth remained.

The Rapacious doesn't seem to fear the tendrils though. But, of course, it wouldn't. The tendrils are merely a manifestation of their incomprehensible appetite. Even as the Rapacious sits near him on the sumptuous sheets, floating free in the void, the monster's stomach growls. They smile.

Their form this time is lean, and their hair is shock white, short, and curly. Their burning eyes are ringed with pink highlights and their skin is as dark as Riverson's own.

Riverson knows that this creature wants to consume him body and soul, but he's turned on anyway; the beast puts on a good show.

"You're awake, love. Good. You overtaxed yourself there. Ruling is hard, isn't it? Let alone a thing as big and voracious as an empire. You're lucky it didn't eat up every little bit of you. But I'm here now, and luckily, I'm easy."

"Where are we?" Riverson asks, moves to the center of the enormous bed knowing that it won't make him any harder to reach when the tendrils come for him. Technically he can see through them, but there's nothing beyond them.

There's only the hunger and the emptiness.

The Rapacious tilts their head flirtatiously. "You're inside me, River. Or, close enough. Remember what I told you about magic in the age of reason? Unspecific. We're somewhere that *I* can reach, and *you* can't easily climb out of." They tap Riverson's nose playfully and bite their lip coquettishly. "So, we can really get to know each other."

"You tricked me so that you could trap me here?"

"Tricked? No. You did exactly what I promised. You blasted those nasty, traitors to pieces and then burned those pieces right up. There's nothing left of them. Bloodlines thousands of years long snuffed out in a blazing moment that will be seen from the far edge of the galaxy once the light catches up. Mmm, it's exciting. *Really* exciting." The Rapacious presses their palms hard into bare thighs. "I just, well…I didn't tell you that you might burn yourself up in the process. But you didn't ask, darling. Anyway, all that is in the past now. You're here and we're together and it's just that…I *know* I said I didn't want to kill you. And I don't! It's just that I'm so hungry, Riv. Do you mind if I take—" Riverson feels the shiver start at his toes and make its way up his spine. He can sense the spectral appendages pressing in. "Just one—" Riverson tries to push his way to the edge of the bed as the Rapacious crawls toward him, bunching the sheets in their coral painted fingertips. "Just a little bite—"

Riverson takes the sheet beneath the monster in both hands and yanks it hard, which sends the Rapacious tumbling off the side of the bed and into the void. In response, one of the tendrils shoots forward, then another. Soon uncountable of the strange, killing arms of the Rapacious are whipping toward him and so he does the only thing he can think of: he leaps.

He falls, but there's no sense of falling. The tendrils follow him down, rushing toward him inexorably. The Rapacious laughs but it sounds like it's coming from everywhere. Their stomach growls and the sound is like war drums. Riverson reaches for the sword that should be at his side, but just as in the real world his hand comes away empty. *One of these days,* he thinks.

And then there's another voice. It says a single word: "Pathetic."

Riverson turns toward the sound and the scene shifts as in a dream, a change that the mind readily accepts. He's standing in his private quarters again and again there is a dead woman on the ground, but this time she is *also* standing beside him: same woman, just not as dead this time. She is stunning in her animated state. The woman's full lips are pressed together, and her tight curls are pulled back away from her faultless dark skin. There's a touch of the void about her, like the Rapacious, who has also come along for the ride.

"Oh," says the dread beast with droll flatness. "She's here."

She gives the monster a look down her broad nose.

"You're me, aren't you? Or, actually, how do I even address you?" Riverson asks the woman.

His—self?—gives him a look as withering as the one she's just given the Rapacious. "*You* may address me as Feast-Empress, Mother of Rivers. You are a failed experiment. A *human* with too much power and too little self-control. Without my memories, you may be more dangerous than the sun-beast itself; at least its lies and manipulations are a known quantity."

"Oh, dearest, nothing is more dangerous than me," replies the Rapacious, baring too white teeth.

The Feast-Empress rolls her head toward them. "Hush, beast, the adults are speaking."

And just like that the Rapacious is gone, disappeared as if it had never been with them. In the logic of this half-dreaming space, Riverson doesn't question the disappearance, but feels a pang of jealous awe at his foremother's capability. She doesn't waste time, returns her attention to him.

"I've banished it. But I doubt it will stay away long now that it's found purchase in your mind. The situation you've found yourself in borders on the apocalyptic." She rubs the bridge of her nose, says as if to herself: "An unbroken line of myself keeps the beast chained and the *one* son threatens to undo all of my—of our—careful work."

Riverson points at her body on the floor. "I didn't ask for this burden. And if you'll recall, it was *your* death that set this into motion."

Her pink eyes are pitiless. "Will they write that in your epitaph? 'Victim of someone else's problems'? Was it not you who allowed the Luperci to fly their ships into Corrected Center space for the first time in our history?"

"I was told…"

"A leader demands good counsel; she is not led by it. You trust the first friendly face you encounter like a domesticated animal on a leash." The Feast-Empress raises a hand to still Riverson's rebuttal before it happens. "Bickering ill befits us. Time is not our friend, even here.

You should have already realized the mechanisms at work. You should already be moving toward resolution."

"I am doing everything within my power," Riverson replies. "In what world is it my fault that you've left me without weapons with which to protect *our* empire? You are here now. *Help* me."

The Feast-Empress looks at him as though she sees something in the lines of his face, a tarot of her own genetics and some new strangeness introduced through magic or circumstance, and it softens her fractionally, as much as such a force of nature can be softened. "It is unfortunate that you are without memories, without trustworthy allies, without a stable galaxy to govern. But you are not powerless. No one of my line ever was or will be, which means that you are not without responsibility. Do not waver. Do not equivocate. Become what everyone around you already thinks you are. Trust in the power of the Feast. Seclude yourself in it, if you must. And do one last thing for me, echo of myself."

"Of course, Feast-Empress."

"Wake up."

Riverson takes a breath and is delighted to find that he is in the corporeal world once more, albeit one where some substantial hell has broken loose.

Celestin has backed away from the fight and a few more members of both the Luperci group and Riverson's own honor guard lie dead. But the real spectacle is that whatever it took to fire the weapon has completely changed the internal consistency of the Corrected Center.

Walls have risen where there were floors, pathways turned counter-clockwise—dumping engineers and dock staff hundreds of feet to their unexpected demise. Where before everything was utilitarian lines, the dock has now become an unstable origami of metal and glass.

Even parts of the Null_Wolf's ship have been integrated into the station's violent shift. The sleek red-black panels fuse with the spartan gray of the Corrected Center to form strange fractal shapes in the floor, and up the walls.

Only the few hundred feet around Riverson in any direction seem to have been spared from this drastic reformation. Unfortunately, this protection seems to have been extended to the Null_Wolf and his troops. The fight, it appears, is still upon them.

And then there's the heat. Riverson believes it is only in his head until he sees that Leeds and Celestin are drenched in sweat as well. Another by-product of the weapon firing then.

His retainer looks at him and brushes a flop of sweaty multi-hued hair out of their face. "You've returned to us, lord. And none too soon. We've suffered some interesting setbacks to the defense of the Corrected Center."

Celestin clenches his teeth, shouts over his shoulder. "Respectfully, Emperor, the entire station just turned into a death machine. What did you do, lord?"

"My duty," Riverson barks. "And I recall that I do not answer to you, General. Now, Leeds: what is the situation with the Luperci fleet?"

"Mostly neutralized from what I can gather. But at least one ship is still capable and incoming. Regretfully, I can find out no more at the moment: the firing of the weapon has unleashed chaos on our internal communications." The retainer works their jaw. "Apparently several dozen of our senior staff have been killed in the abrupt reconfiguration of the station: ejected into space, trapped within sudden walls, incinerated in the conflagration. Also, the Cloud's End Cult representative has been killed; I've taken the liberty of removing the meeting from your schedule. "Riverson needs a moment to take this in, but the Null_Wolf and the rest of the Luperci are still coming and despite the decimation of their fleet and the deaths in their ranks, the Luperci shows no sign of backing down. Worse still, Riverson can see the Rapacious standing just

behind the Null_Wolf. This time she's dressed in a gown
of flowing blood and wearing a bone diadem—a ring of
metacarpals fastidiously holding her coif in place. She
smiles a smile just for Riverson.

"We'll fall back to the Feast Hall," Riverson says.
"I need to return to the Feast, and I imagine it's more
defensible."

He doesn't mention the advice of the previous Feast-
Empress or that the Rapacious tried to consume him; he
already has one group trying to remove him. But Leeds,
sharp-eyed as ever, follows Riverson's gaze to what must
seem to be an empty space over the Null_Wolf's shoulder.
The First-Retainer doesn't comment.

The process of falling back from the fight is complicated
by several factors: the relative skill of the Luperci fighters
is one and the other is the transfiguration of the Corrected
Center. The elevator shaft is now a sort of impressionistic
version of itself: a pillar of jutting metal, useless for its
intended purpose. However, toward the sunward side of
the platform is a freshly-made, sharp-angled aggregate of
metal that forms what seems to be a relatively stable shelf.
It juts between the platform and the ground at roughly
a 45° angle. One of the surviving members of Riverson's
honor-guard points it out as a potential egress before
throwing herself back into the fight.

Alongside Celestin, there are three remaining members
of Riverson's honor guard. They're armed with hand-
cannons firing hot plasma and swords that prove to be
much more than the ornamental weapons that Riverson
took them for. As the soldiers on Riverson's side clash
with the Luperci, the emperor and Leeds take to the
narrow, ad hoc walkway and begin to descend. As he
takes cautious steps down the steep band of bizarrely fused
metal, Riverson is acutely aware of how high up he is and
very relieved to find out that he's not particularly afraid of
heights.

However, behind him, he hears Leeds mumbling a steady litany of tightly coiled words: a charm, or a fervent wish, or a prayer.

"We're almost there, Leeds. Keep your head," Riverson says. He couches the reassurance in the tone of an order, trusting that Leeds will respond better to the call of duty than to personal appeal. His gambit seems to work because Leeds's utterances soften and their footsteps quicken.

They reach solid ground before long. When Leeds exits the pathway behind him, the First-Retainer looks a little harried and clearly grateful to be off the precarious slab of metal.

"Doing alright, Leeds?" Riverson asks.

"Perfectly, lord. Well…close enough."

"Close enough is good; I've made do with less in my extremely short life."

Leeds—improbably paler than their baseline—just nods.

Riverson looks up to where his forces are still skirmishing, though now falling back toward the walkway. The honor-guard member who showed them the path is struck down and the other two form a barrier so that Celestin can safely retreat. Even from this distance, Riverson can tell that the general is galled to be protected by foot soldiers, but when he looks over his shoulder at Riverson with only the First-Retainer by his side, the general turns and takes the sloped walkway at speed, running down its slanted side at a terrifying pace. It's the kind of heroic and ridiculous act that songs are written about, except that when he nears the ground, he's going too fast and ends up slipping at the very end. To save himself from breaking his neck, the general springs up into a leaping arc and hits the ground in a roll. He hisses as he half tumbles out of it and goes ass over elbows.

He finds his way to standing quickly enough though and in his hand is one of the plasma-cannons. He aims it at the impromptu walkway and with three well-placed shots he collapses it.

"That won't stop a Luperci strike force from coming after us. We have to go, Emperor," Celestin says.

Riverson agrees and within a few seconds they're moving. The emperor tries not to think about the fact that they've left the other guards to fight and to die.

But as they pass the bodies of people consumed by the weapon that Riverson unleashed in this internecine squabble, the death toll gets harder for him to ignore. Their greatly diminished group moves through a station made strange by the Corrected Center's inhuman modifications, the missing crew, and other horrors.

Leeds matches Riverson step-for-step as they traverse the alien geometries of the reconfigured hallways, stepping over fractal explosions of organic and inorganic matter; there are corpses embedded in the walls. Some of them still breathe.

The first that they pass is an older man with a distinguished face, or what remains of one. "General... soldier..." He croaks with the part of his mouth that still moves, that isn't the ceiling or the wall. "Please."

Celestin takes several deep breaths, hardens himself, and searches for the part of the man's body that's still flesh, where his mind might reside despite the cruel restructuring that has distributed him randomly throughout the hall. Celestin unsheathes his blade and says something in a language that Riverson doesn't understand as he drives it into the ground, into the man's heart. It might've been a curse word or a prayer.

The general ends other lives just as mercifully, but there are too many to save. Eventually, the group has to move on.

As they maneuver these awful hallways, Leeds says, "Emperor, this is not the opportune time, but I fear with the problems stacking there may never be another opportunity. I feel we should discuss your...possible insanity."

Riverson—who has nearly been consumed by a monster only he can see, was admonished by his dead former self, and presides over an orgy required for the continuance of the galaxy—doesn't flinch. "What of it?"

"It might be prudent for you to be liquidated. There are protocols for imperials who have likely been compromised by the Rapacious, though we've never deployed them. It can be done painlessly, and you would most likely be replaced immediately."

Riverson's *no* constitutes the entirety of his side of the conversation. Celestin looks surprised.

"Emperor, if you are compromised—" the general begins.

"No," Riverson says again. He stops walking and addresses both his companions. "I woke on this station to utter confusion, to a situation that has somehow become even murkier and more dangerous than when I was *murdered* today. I cannot potentially thrust this situation into the hands of someone even less capable of unfucking it, and I will not be made to. Am I understood?"

Both Celestin and Leeds affirm this verbally and their little group continues winding through the arteries of the station. Somewhere beyond Riverson can hear the laughter of the Rapacious, and knows that the Null_Wolf stalks their steps; Riverson quickens his.

BACK AT THE heart of the Feast, Riverson's first order of business is to demand a damned blade.

The amber strobe of emergency lights washes over the Feast, but its geometry has remained blessedly unchanged. The frenetic pace of the seething bodies has taken on a hushed, halting note. Lovers pause to check in with shaking partners, distracted organs soften and must be coaxed again to fullness with suggestions of delight beyond measure, as if any pleasure within the fullness of human reckoning had not, at some point, already made an appearance at the Feast.

The ringleader of this insatiable horde sits on the black glass throne and strokes his chin.

Leeds and Celestin are off to one side of the elevated command platform speaking in hushed, pointed tones, and the number of fawning officials has halved. Riverson listens carefully. He hears the noises of the oversexed mob, but he doesn't hear the Rapacious. *A fucking mercy,* he thinks.

"General Celestin," the emperor calls.

Celestin gives Leeds a hard look, ending their conversation, and approaches his liege. He bows but says nothing.

"I'm sorry that you lost people. How many Perpetual Front ships remain?"

"Not enough. The initial fight took down half my squad. Your...attack cost more." Celestin's face is a complete blank. "Maybe a half dozen ships total."

"Not enough," Riverson says to himself. He calls out to a communications tech. One of few remaining apparently. "How many Luperci dropships?"

"Only one, my liege. But they'll likely have enough manpower to field a considerable boarding force and they're already in the river."

Riverson nods, slides his coral gaze back to Celestin. "We'll give your remaining ships coordinates to navigate the river. Have your crew chase them and continue to harrying their flank. Buy us time."

Celestin's eyes narrow. His anger is visible and rising. "To what end? The rest of the Front is too far out to rescue us. The Luperci dropship, when it finishes navigating the protective field, contains too many of their soldiers for us to hold off. How does more bloodshed help the Staghead Empire?"

Riverson rises from the throne and unfolds himself to full height. He finds that he's taller than Celestin by a hair. But his size, his breadth, doesn't come from anything so mundane as that. He takes a single step forward and the Feast surges; cries of ecstasy drown out his footfalls. "I *am* the empire, General. And you forget yourself."

Celestin takes a half-step back and falls to one knee. His mouth forms a probable apology, but Riverson doesn't hear it. In fact, he can't hear anything besides the groans of the participants in the Feast. Again, he feels the pull of it against his mind. It would be so easy to slide into it and let the all-consuming thrill it promises wash over him, leaving nothing beside the needy, sensuous self. But thinking about sex and hunger makes him think of the Rapacious and thinking about the beast's reddened lips parted in delight calls the red-black wolf's mask to mind. He takes a breath and returns to himself.

"Understand," Riverson says, addressing the entire room, "that we are in a battle for the heart of our empire, and it is not lost on me that a person or persons close to the throne has betrayed it. If each one of you is not prepared to give everything you have, everything you are to this fight, then you are an enemy of the Staghead Empire. Until the corruption is rooted out, leniency is off the table."

Everything goes quiet aside from the wet noises of the Feast. Confident that he's more than adequately made his point, Riverson moves on. "Leeds."

The retainer appears and Riverson looks at their half-toned hair and bland, neutral expression. Riverson considers the first moments of his own instantiation and Leeds's guidance. He also thinks of the Feast-Empress's guidance: *A leader demands good counsel; she is not led by it.*

"Do you still think I should—what was the word?—
liquidate myself?"

Leeds bows. "I do, my liege. If your inability to
remember is a temporary aberration, then having your
subsequent instance appear could remedy quite a few of
the current problems facing the Corrected Center."

"Understand something then: I am the emperor, and
my body and spirit are inviolable. Injury done to me
is injury done to the empire itself. We will deal with
the traitorous Luperci and then you and I will have a
conversation about what you imagine the exact goals of
your counsel ought to be."

Leeds doesn't so much as flinch, but something about
the immediate sharpness of their body language suggests
that the armor of formality has been raised in defense.
However, their ruffled feathers are the least of Riverson's
concerns. There's increased chatter and noise at the huge
double doors at the entrance of the feast hall. Riverson
takes a short, sharp breath and waits for the inevitable.

The door buckles inward with a shock of force, another
bows the heavy wood and steel further, and a third takes
the reinforced double doors off their hinges.

The Null_Wolf takes his first steps into the heart of
the Feast. He is alone and his beautifully lacquered mask
is cracked on the left side so that not just his dark eye,
but also the smooth skin of his cheek is revealed. Behind
him, the guards lie dead alongside a number of Luperci
soldiers.

Fabian takes a moment to look around at the Feast, but
his gaze soon narrows in on Riverson. Celestin once again
throws himself in front of the emperor and brandishes his
blade.

"Emperor. You've led me on a merry chase—and I
concede that your fuck palace is fine, indeed—however, I
think it's past time for us to conclude this thing. Don't you
think?"

The Null_Wolf takes a few steps into the Feast Hall and Riverson is proud to see that many of the hangers-on standing on the dais doing inscrutable work, whom he'd taken for political flotsam, arm themselves and race toward the Luperci's murderous son. The Null_Wolf removes them from the mortal coil without breaking a sweat. Celestin holds his position and his sword level, breathing slowly and evenly as Fabian takes a few more steps forward.

"General Celestin, I look forward to clashing swords with you again. The empire should be honored to have your service. I am sorry that your troops were felled. I fear those continuing to engage with my brothers will meet a similar fate, but not for a lack of valor. You were simply at the wrong place at the wrong time," says Fabian.

Celestin presses his lips together, nods. "I have spent a lifetime at the end of the galaxy, fighting supposed outsiders and defending the empire against invented threats. I have taken lives, I have stolen resources, I have bled, and I have spilled blood for the empire." He takes another deep breath, spins on his heel, and thrusts his sword into Riverson's body.

The general aims for the chest, but Riverson moves and the blade catches his side instead. It slides in so easily, so cleanly, that Riverson struggles to make sense of it. He notes the evenness of Celestin's gaze and Leeds's mild expression.

Conspiracy, then, Riverson thinks over the howl of pain arriving all at once.

Celestin pushes the blade deeper. "Perhaps we do not deserve this bounty, my liege, when we bloody everything we touch."

The Null_Wolf holds his blade aloft, as if frozen in the moment. "Oh. Wasn't expecting that."

The emperor tries to speak, finds that he can't—there's an expanding ocean of pain in the way. The pain is clean and copious, annoying in its capacity to distract. There is a galaxy in peril and a dread beast fitfully slumbering in the sun and a conspiracy against his rule and now he has a *fucking sword in his side*!

When Riverson breathes a raspy, rattling breath and reaches for the blade, Celestin leans on it, pushing it through him and coming in close as a lover. Riverson can smell the general's sweat over the coppery tang of his own blood.

Riverson struggles again to push words between his lips, but instead there is just a frail groan.

As he collapses, things get truly interesting.

First, he can feel the hesitance of the Feast. The frenetic energy of the undulating bodies seizes all at once and in that instance, the Rapacious appears. He is no longer subdued or demure. He leans in from over Celestin's shoulder and to Riverson's surprise, the general seems to be able to briefly perceive the monster.

Celestin says something to the beast, but Riverson doesn't catch it; he is fading quickly. The beast smiles.

My turn, the Rapacious mouths. It blinks out of existence then reappears floating somewhere over the Feast Hall. Both arms spread wide and from the body of the beast blooms a myriad ravenous, searching, killing tendrils.

They explode in every direction and wherever they touch flesh that flesh is gone, consumed more hungrily than even fire which has the grace at least to leave smoke in its wake. The tendrils *are* hunger, and they wend through the Feast hall, turning the bodies they find into a banquet more awful than any that has ever been staged in this august space.

The first to be consumed are swallowed too rapidly for fear to overtake them, but those blissful ends don't last. There are screams and the terrifying press of bodies as the Feast turns into a crush. Terror narrows reason into animal instinct: *Escape. Escape. Escape.*

The tendrils, incorporeal and visible only to their bearer and to a rapidly fading Riverson, have no fear of the vacuum of space and they reach out in every direction. The oncoming Luperci ship, in the middle of its careful navigation through the Corrected Center protective field, is taken unawares. Thousands are dispatched in a terrible instant that in the memories of the survivors will become endless.

Even the pilots of the remaining ships of the Perpetual Front, the people for whom Celestin would give his own life, are consumed. The tendrils seek only the warmth of flesh, so once they are swallowed up, their ships are left unscathed and drift like toys abandoned by careless hands.

And within the riven hall where the emperor bleeds, all at once, in a single, mournful voice: the Feast wails.

ACT III

HUNGRY
IS THE
CROWN

RIVERSON HAS NEVER seen so much blood, which is saying something. One might expect that a man come to consciousness mere moments after his own assassination would have seen the worst wound possible. He puts pressure to his side and his hand runs crimson surprisingly quickly, a bad sign he suspects. But aside from the possibility of bleeding to death, there is also the question of the end times.

The Rapacious's attack has decimated the Feast. The profusion of beautiful bodies has been thinned and those that remain cling to each other in wide-eyed fear, their passions curdled in the traumatic upheaval. Riverson doubts that many of them ever truly considered the consequences of failing to hold back the slumbering beast. The monster might have been secondary to their political and social ambitions, but now they have seen that their work is more essential than they knew; he pities them the horrible realization that the pleasure they manufacture is a kind of cage, and not just for the Rapacious. Some of the survivors kiss hesitantly, stroke trembling shoulders, perhaps trying to find their way back to their duty knowing the awesome consequences should they fail again—or maybe this service is all that they know and a balm in incomprehensible times.

The amber emergency lights continue to flash; they frame Celestin as he stands at the center of the dais with his blade in hand, dripping the empire's most precious fluid. The general's expression is firm, grim. His bright eyes seem lost and haunted in the strobe. He turns slowly to where Riverson is crouched, breathing raggedly, and trying to stay conscious.

Celestin continues a one-sided conversation. "And why *should* it survive? An empire built on the backs of people it cares nothing for. A figurehead standing at the shore, bargaining with the flood. You act as though all this belongs to you, but the blood that moistens the gears is not your own, Emperor." He looks at Leeds. "And you…"

Leeds.

The First-Retainer is standing off to one side with their arms wrapped around their midsection, chin tucked. A little beatific grin blooms on their mouth. "As I've explained, General, this is how it was meant to be. So much work went into this moment. All the threads of magic I've dutifully plucked apart over the years of my faithful service. Just to create even the slimmest *chance* of producing a broken incarnation."

Celestin sneers. "You're no better than the bastard emperor that you're trying to usurp."

"No, you're right. We all reduce ourselves in service to the empire. All the wonders of all the worlds cannot excuse our reliance on placating a hungry mouth. Our divine whore of an emperor makes a bed of himself to buy us time, but there is never enough time. That-which-eats will never be satisfied until it has consumed all. We should invite this just conclusion. It's a glorious end that we are unworthy of. An arc of redemption for a perverse empire built on bones and semen."

"I told you before: I want justice. I'm not interested in your death cult," Celestin seethes.

"You're an instrument of its will just the same," Leeds replies.

The dais has been cleared by the Rapacious's attack; the only other player remaining on the stage is the Null_ Wolf. His mask lies in halves at his feet, and he crouches, suffering perhaps from some unseen wound. Though he says nothing, when Celestin takes a step toward the emperor, Fabian launches into action. He dashes across the dais and throws himself into a roll that ends with him bouncing upright with his sword flashing in between Celestin and Riverson.

Celestin hesitates.

"Here." Fabian tosses something back to the Feast-Emperor. "Put that on your wound. Combat stim. Witch-made. Slap it on and fight through the pain. Then fight for real, if you can," Fabian says. He keeps his gaze on Celestin, who is circling him and ready to take advantage of any distraction.

Riverson takes the pack, does as he's told. The Null_ Wolf is right: it is not pleasant. However, he feels better almost immediately despite the searing pain racing up his side and the sudden pounding throb in his head. "Why are you protecting me?"

Fabian doesn't answer, not immediately. Celestin comes in with an exploratory strike. Fabian parries, leaps back, makes sure to keep himself positioned in front of Riverson. "Damnit, Emperor, I want to stabilize the galaxy! Instead, I've played a role in bringing it to its knees." He shakes his head. "I can't communicate with the dropship; I fear my brothers are dead. Which means I currently have as many loyal allies in the Corrected Center as you do."

"Traitor turns rescuer. Do you think that will save you from the axe man, Null_Wolf?" Riverson asks.

"Frankly, that's a lot of mouth considering only one of us has a hole in his side. Sit still now, sweet emperor; daddy has a little blood to spill." Fabian says, then winks at Celestin.

But the general was unfazed by the other swordsman's games. "Null_Wolf. Step aside. We've both lost people to this pointless conflict. We do not need to continue someone else's fight."

Fabian flicks his wrist to flash his blade once more. "You and I have nothing in common, General. You are rabble, an up-jumped commoner led by the nose into an attempt on the life of the emperor. You're a joke with no punchline. If you have something to say, say it with your blade."

Celestin's shoulders sag slightly. "Conflict it is."

They move. It's as if their fight before was a mere prelude to this moment. Their swords spark as they come together. Fabian is swift and aggressive, Celestin, smooth and stalwart. They dance around the dais, clashing and trading ground. The winner is clear only for a moment before the circumstance pivots—often on a minor change in stance, a parry that seems serendipitous but comes out of long practice, or a beautiful bit of footwork—and the outcome of the situation becomes murky again.

The two of them perform this dance accompanied by hushed voices, stifled moans, and the sounds of the skittish, injured Feast tentatively rousing itself once again. As he feels the rising tide of the Feast, Riverson briefly considers calling out to its participants, getting them to join the fight, but he can also tell how fragile it is. He cannot spare even a single soul, so he stands despite the pain in his side and as Leeds approaches him, brandishes their sword: a long, curved blade.

"Why do you refuse to do what your forebears are so good at and *die*, Emperor?" Leeds asks. "So much delicate work has gone into this moment. So many lives expended to get the axis of this galaxy tilted just enough to make you vulnerable. So much done to override the Luperci's hesitance to act, to arrange for your murder, to put Celestin's sword in your gut." The First-Retainer raises their blade in Riverson's direction. "Everything hangs by a thread. The Rapacious haunts your steps. If you die now, all will end as it was meant to."

Riverson draws his own weapon and unfolds to his full height. He reaches one hand to his side to check on his wound. It's tender still, but now closed. That'll have to be enough.

"By whom?" Riverson asks neutrally.

"Pardon me, Emperor?" Leeds replies, genuinely confused.

"All would end as it meant to, you said. But by whom? On whose authority would you cut me down? The galaxy's? Your death cult's? Or your own?" Riverson takes a few steps forward, the heat of indignation rolling inside him. "I will accept nothing less than your best, Leeds. You want your apocalypse so bad?" Riverson shifts his weight onto his back heel, steadies his arm, and lengthens his reach. "Come take it."

To their credit, Leeds doesn't hesitate. They lash out hard and fast, revealing themself to be a trained fighter. Riverson is driven back by the unexpectedly fierce opening, but recovers quickly. Leeds is a true believer and they fight with a believer's zeal. Their eyes are bright, slightly mad with fervor as they slash again and again. Riverson meets each blow capably and keeps the boundaries of the dais in mind as he's forced to yield ground. His body knows its way around a sword, but the full weight of his skills are slower to rouse—he can see the perfect cut in his mind's eye, but his limbs are just a moment too slow, and by the time his sword goes where it's supposed to be, Leeds has already moved.

Across from them a bit further down the raised pathway, Celestin and Fabian's fight has devolved into a messy brawl. Blood freely drips to the pristine floor—it could belong to either.

Meanwhile, arriving in a storm of golden petals is the Rapacious. Seemingly choosing the exact worst moment, it reappears after its meal of human souls as a thickly built demi-human shape with several mouths bedecked in gold from head to toe. Riverson can only spare a glance; light glints off the luminous rings running through the monster's nipples. It parts its lips to reveal golden teeth. Riverson shudders and the Feast experiences a collective bodily tremor.

"You fight like you aim to live, River. Why not consider the alternative?" the Rapacious asks.

Leeds maintains their edge, but Riverson feels his muscles loosening, his steps getting faster. He lashes out with a kick to Leeds's knee, trying to reduce their speed. The kick connects, but lower than expected and drives instead into the meat of Leeds's calf. They snarl, refocus, come at him eagain.

"Death doesn't have to be terror, Feast-Emperor," the Rapacious speaks over their swordplay. "If you let me consume you, if you give yourself over, then I will burn away the ties that keep you bound to this universe in an endless loop. You will become more than a mere plaything of your witch ancestress. I will swallow you up and inside me you will be doused in pleasure. All of you will be a slow burning eruption. Eternity can be pleasure and consumption. We will eat the stars and drench the darkness in ecstasy."

Riverson hears the words, can't help but feel the tug of lust. More than just a fragment of him wants what the monster is offering.

Elsewhere, Fabian is fighting hard as well; he drips sweat and sports new bruises and cuts. And though Celestin appears, at last, to be the heartier of the two, Riverson is too occupied with the person trying to kill him to help Fabian. Besides, he doesn't think that the Null_ Wolf's pride would suffer it if he did. Instead the Feast-

Emperor throws all he has into his fight with Leeds.

As it turns out, that doesn't appear to be quite enough. Though Riverson feels like he's gaining ground, his calm and collected First-Retainer's desperate, harried strikes suddenly become relaxed and powerful. Riverson's hopes that he was exhausting Leeds evaporate, and it becomes obvious that Leeds was baiting him into expending more energy than he could afford. The emperor tries not to clutch his wound, though he can now feel it again bleeding freely. His head is woozy and he struggles to stay in his fighting stance.

"Tired, love? Come rest your head on my bosom," the Rapacious coos. "Oh, forgot it. I'll just use your head as a handsome footstool once the traitor separates it from your body."

At this stage, the First-Retainer's perfectly neat outfit is slashed and one toned arm hangs free of it. Their hair is a mess and their eyes sad. "I don't delight in this. I take no pleasure from it. But I must cut you down."

Their swords come together again and this time, Leeds's eyes go wide. Riverson has found something, something indelible, inside himself. He feels a surge in his chest and a chorus of sighs erupts from the Feast. He pivots, releases himself from the clash, and comes back at Leeds so ferociously that the First-Retainer stumbles. Riverson hears his pulse, but it's not his pulse: it's the pulse of every naked, writhing body in the room and their power, their cumulative, serotonin-addled spirits feed him. Riverson feasts on them all and he grins as he fights.

"Less talking then, more slicing," Riverson says.

Leeds is forced to fall back. They're capable and skilled, but what they're fighting is no longer a neophyte emperor with a broken mind, but the living agent of the Feast, a force strong enough to hold back the inevitable itself. Leeds is fighting the very power that dams the flood and they're losing.

Ultimately, with a series of flourishes, Riverson knocks the curved blade from Leeds's hand and puts his shorter blade to their throat.

"You lose," Riverson says.

Leeds looks tired, beaten, as if this were just a footnote in the long record of their defeats. "No, my lord. We all lose."

Riverson doesn't have time to wallow in his First-Retainer's fatalism. Instead, he kicks Leeds off of the dais and into the Feast. With a thought, the emperor commands his ecstatic servants to restrain his freshly murderous attendant.

The other duel is similarly coming to an end and not the one Riverson hopes for. Fabian is on his knees, there's blood at his crown and ugly gashes down his arms. His left arm in particular hangs badly. Celestin has sustained injuries as well, but not nearly as many.

"We've both tried, in our ways, to change this galaxy, Fabian. But this—" the general gestures to the opulence around them, the decadence, "—all this is a monument to the same hungers this empire purports to fight. Will you not—"

Fabian growls: "Pass!" He lunges forward with a knife pulled from his boot and stabs Celestin in the thigh. The general shouts, would answer with his sword, but Fabian stays low, wraps an arm around Celestin's injured leg and yanks him off his feet. The general crashes into the dais hip first and the Null_Wolf slides his bloody knife to Celestin's throat. The tip eases into the skin gently, slowly. Blood flows.

"Good night, General," Fabian says, poised to end Celestin's life. "You deserved better."

"Stop," Riverson commands.

Fabian can't hide his surprise. "I'm sorry, what?"

"If we murder everyone who means the throne ill this whole station would be littered with corpses. Well, more corpses." Riverson gives the Null_Wolf a pointed look. "Or are you prepared to turn that blade on yourself afterward?"

Fabian cocks his head to the side. He stands and stretches out his long lean-muscled body, but never takes his eyes off of Celestin. Eventually he shrugs. "As you wish, Emperor. General? Stand. Slowly, please."

The Null_Wolf takes his time binding Celestin's arms behind him with some sort of magnetic lock that proves even more complicated than it initially looks. Over his shoulder, Riverson hears the whisper, and turns toward the Rapacious: "Bravo. You've conquered the insurrection. How they'll rave about you in the history texts, Emperor. Oh. Wait. There won't be any history, will there? Once I break loose and swallow every single world that has ever developed a writing system. It's a victory in name only. So many lie dead and soon many more will vanish into me. Just thinking about it excites me beyond reason."

Riverson frowns. The monster, for all its horrible appetite, is no fool. When Riverson surveys the thrusting, sighing bodies remaining in the Feast he can feel the energy being generated and it's not enough. The maw inside the sun is groaning, stretching—it tests the strength of its bonds with every sigh and finds them weaker by the moment. Riverson is running out of options, which the Rapacious, grinning at him from the edge of his vision, can only know all too well.

The emperor makes his way over to Fabian who has both hands on his hips and stares out at the burning sun.

"So much trouble from a ball of gas and fire, eh?" says the Null_Wolf, when Riverson doesn't laugh, Fabian lets his smile melt. "If you're expecting an apology, you'll have a long wait, my lord. The situation in the galaxy is tense. The rebellions...we couldn't overlook potential weakness in the leadership of the empire."

"So you thought you could slide in and put your name on the marquee?" Riverson retorts.

Fabian mimes a kiss, insouciant to the last. "And my face. Don't forget about my face, Emperor."

"I promise you, I haven't. In fact, I think the empire may have a use for it. That mouth of yours, in particular."

"Oh? Do tell. I'm a fine orator."

"We have to join the Feast. You and I."

"Naturally, Emperor. I'll do anything—" Fabian is already halfway through his reply to the sentence before he hears it. "Wait. Hold a moment. The Feast? As in?" He points. "Me?"

Riverson blinks at the warrior whose blush rises hard and fast. Elsewhere, Fabian rises even quicker and just as hard.

"If this is a question of preference—" Riverson begins.

Fabian waves his hands, turns redder. "What? No. I...I *prefer* just fine, thank you, Emperor. I just...why me?"

"Luperci. You have a pure bloodline. You can trace it back to one of the witches who were at the foundation of the empire, who sprung the trap that sealed the beast. I represent the blood as well. Directly. I've learned a little bit about rituals since my incarnation and the blood we carry has deep power. Look, I don't have time to look for a better option, Fabian," Riverson replies shortly.

"I understand. It's just...Emperor..."

"River," the Feast-Emperor replies, smiles to project absent levity. "We're about to get very close, very quickly. River is fine. I've only ever been called that by a monster who lives in the sun, so I'd very much like to reclaim the nickname, if possible. Especially if we fuck this up and die as a result."

"All right then: River. That's so fucking strange..." Fabian runs a hand through his dark hair. "How do we begin?"

Riverson looks out into the void and at the burning, pitiless sun. "First, we close the hole in my side. After that? Honestly? I have no idea. But I know who might."

The Feast-Empress doesn't seem surprised to have been called from beyond the grave or that her protégé has unlocked this new ability. For a specter, she's fairly calm. She turns her pink rose-hued eyes on Riverson, flicks them across Fabian, and then takes in the Feast. "A disaster, then."

Riverson nods and points toward the sun. Spectral tendrils that only Riverson—and presumably the empress—can see are starting to tentatively reach out of it. "A disaster. Unprecedented, probably."

The empress taps a finger on her chin. "Empire is a series of concurrent calamities. Project a little steel, a little grace, and you'd be surprised what people will move past. Especially when you're in charge of how the story will be recorded into history." She shrugs. "Assuming that the Rapacious doesn't eat all of the known worlds. Now, why, exactly, am I here?"

"I need to join the Feast."

"Personally?" She looks aghast.

"We're running out of bodies."

The revels have taken on a funereal air: the slow, a-rhythmic humping of the emotionally ravaged. The sensation that answers this sight is buried within Riverson's chest: it's a sort of non-specific sunward tug, as if the Rapacious were trying to drag him and the station around him into its fiery embrace. "And we don't have much time," Riverson adds.

The empress shakes her head. "And your partner for this…excursion?"

Riverson inclines his head toward the Null_Wolf, who waves, ostensibly at the empress, but since he can't see the spectral ruler, he gestures toward open air. The empress winces.

"The result of hundreds of years of selective breeding and…that's the result."

"He's better with a sword in hand," Riverson says.

Fabian's perfect brow crinkles at that. "Is the empress slandering me?"

"Hush," Riverson and the empress say simultaneously. Even though Fabian only hears Riverson, he looks appropriately chastened.

The empress straightens, which is not to suggest that her posture was ever anything less than fully rigid. "This is going to require some calibration, descendant. You were built for rule. Every fiber of your being is meant to impose order on chaos. Descending into animal lust has been… strongly discouraged. In fact, to show any weakness has not been our way, even before my sisters and I snared the beast.

"However, circumstances have taught us to be flexible above all. So, I'm sure you'll figure it out."

Riverson's laugh comes out a touch hysterical. "Wait, so none of us have ever…never?"

The Feast-Empress's smile is small, secret. Riverson leaves it alone. "Fine, okay, how do I start?"

"As all desire starts: delectation."

Riverson looks at Fabian and attempts to *see* him. There is the posture: calculated looseness hiding coiled power, always at the ready for immediate violence. Riverson tries to picture the muscles tensing and shifting beneath his dark armor, imagines how those muscles might be used for something besides extraordinarily efficient murder…

"How do people do this?" Riverson asks, folds his arms across his chest, then, fidgeting, uncurls one arm to point at Fabian. "He's a soldier, a killer, not some nubile supplicant."

"Hey!" Fabian says.

Both Riverson and his forebear ignore the Null_Wolf. The empress continues, "Everyone is more than the sum of their parts. Or do you imagine that it will be easy for *him* to view *you* as a desirous creature rather than the chain keeping the sun from devouring everything? Especially since you're covered in your own blood."

"Surprisingly, Empress, that does not help," Riverson remarks.

"Then help yourself. Focus, descendant. Or have you found some extra time in your back pocket?"

Riverson ignores that last quip, and tries again to focus on Fabian. He supposes he has very nice shoulders, or at least he supposes that Fabian has nice shoulders underneath his armor, his ridiculous armor.

"Can you take that off? You know, undress?" Riverson asks. He tries to keep his voice neutral, but even he can hear the irritation.

"Naturally, Emperor," Fabian replies. His tone is clipped as he begins to undo the seals that keep his impressive black protective garments intact. He winces as he lowers his armor over his left arm. Riverson's reflex is to touch the badly bruised arm, but he doubts himself, just as he doubts that Fabian's frustration is an auspicious start to their coupling. Yet, he has to admit that as the actual shape of Fabian's body emerges from beneath its glittering shell: there's something there.

The Null_Wolf wears a simple shirt of a peculiar weave and long-sleeves underneath his armor; it's doused in his sweat. And for some reason it's the sweat, rather than the blood he's so far shed, that makes Riverson begin to think of him as human.

"Your hair?" Riverson says, more quietly than he intends.

Perhaps Fabian is feeling the start of something himself, because the irritation on his face softens to a mild confusion, or is that amusement? He reaches up and undoes the clasp around his high, tight ponytail and his hair falls down. River exhales. The dark hair makes his hooded eyes less piercing, his square jaw more...inviting?

"Your turn, River. Come here," Fabian says.

Riverson raises an eyebrow at the command, but he can see the empress in the corner of his vision. She mouths a word: *flexible*. Riverson takes a few steps toward Fabian, who blinks at him when he stops several feet away. Riverson inhales deeply and takes the remaining steps to put him within arm span.

"You were sent here to kill me. I hope you appreciate that this is a significant investment in trust," Riverson says.

"Please." Fabian rolls his eyes. "I was sent to *depose* you. Murder was a last resort."

"Somehow that doesn't put me at ease, Null_Wolf."

"Oh, you need to be at ease now? I thought this was—"

There's a noise of general alarm and terror as one of the tendrils of the Rapacious erupts through the ground and through the chest of a feast-participant. The man's mouth parts in a shape that could be pain or rapture. His eyes become glassy and he's gone instantly. The people around him are understandably unsettled. There's screaming and panic throughout the Feast, which Riverson feels in his chest like an immense throbbing pressure, like a physical blow repeating.

Fabian catches him before he realizes that he's falling.

"The protections are getting weaker. The Rapacious is getting closer," Riverson tells him.

Fabian instinctively looks up at the burning sun, as though he might see something crawling from it, but

there is nothing but the same boiling heat and gas. As
Fabian searches for an enemy to fight, Riverson focuses
on keeping the Feast from breaking down. He steadies
his breathing to soothe his racing heart. Despite himself,
he feels a fraction safer in the arms of a man who would
likely have shed few tears over killing him.

Fabian scans the emperor's face. "River. Explain what's
going on so I can help."

Riverson swallows, tries to speak, but the growing
requirements of the Feast interfere with every aspect of
his thinking. The wound in his side doesn't help. "I am
the Feast. It feeds me and I feed it. If either of us falter,
everything dies."

"Then let me take care of the physical part. Relax,
focus on…whatever it is you have to focus on. And I'll do
the rest," Fabian says, lowering them both to the ground.

"Leave the survival of the galaxy to you?"

"What choice do you have?" Fabian asks.

"What choice, indeed," adds the empress. Riverson
looks over at her and this time she's sitting the throne,
looking more effortlessly regal than Riverson ever has,
likely ever will. "The egg is cracked, descendant. For a
myriad years my efforts have kept it still. Now, it's your
turn. I couldn't have sealed it without help. Neither can
you."

Riverson grunts. He's been emperor for less than a day
and several millennia of quotidian existence have fully,
simultaneously unraveled. Though his pride is hardwired,
Riverson can no more imperiously stare down the end of
the all things than Fabian can run a sword through it.

"All right, Null_Wolf—"

"We're about to get intimate, you can call me Fabian."

Someone in the Feast starts weeping hysterically and
Riverson feels their anguish sweep over him. "Intimate.
Yes. You should know, Fabian. I don't think I've ever…
been a participant."

"Wait, what?"

"My forebears, it's… it's been beneath us."

"Fuck, I get it. I get it. So I'm going to break in the Emperor? It feels like a capital crime."

Riverson gives Fabian an exhausted smile. His eyes are narrowed as the fractured Feast causes his head to pound like a pick through his frontal lobe. "Luckily you're already a traitor to the throne. Show me a good time and maybe I'll pardon you."

"Respectfully, River. Shut up," Fabian says, and then presses his lips to Riverson's. The importance of intimate contact is a part of the Feast-Emperor's duty and his DNA, woven through his understanding of himself and the world, but he finds there's a difference between the encyclopedic carnal knowledge that shouts in his blood and the specific tenderness of *this* man's lips against *his*.

And then, immediately there's the terror. As Fabian nibbles against his lower lip and begins to tease Riverson's mouth open with the very tip of his tongue, Riverson realizes that the kiss, the sensation, has become the center of his attention. He holds his breath a little waiting for the next development. The weight of the Feast begins to burn off of him like morning dew and he reaches desperately for it, wrests control. Someone on the other side of the Feast hall collapses.

"You're tensing up," Fabian whispers, rubs Riverson's shoulders and goes back for another kiss. Riverson pulls away slightly, flinches.

"I can't…"

Fabian hands stop kneading and he pulls away. "This is new for the both of us, in different ways I'm sure. But…"

"If I lose focus, we die."

"If we don't do this, we die anyway," Fabian says.

"You don't understand."

"I don't. But I understand the sprawl of responsibility, the depth of it. And I know that you can't meet your fate piecemeal. Sometimes you have to just jump."

"That's easy for you to say," Riverson says. Another presence fades from the Feast and Riverson can't tell whether it's the Rapacious or anguish that has claimed them. "This is everything, Fabian."

"Then let me shoulder some of it. Let me help you."

Riverson glances again at the empress. She's no longer on the throne, she's standing at the very edge of the raised dais closest to its sunward edge. Her hands are clasped behind her back and she stares at the sun. "So many of my lives have gone to this. I ask myself how many more are owed and the answer appears to be: all of them." She shakes her head. "I was wrong to treat you as separate from myself. Let us remedy that now."

She doesn't turn back, so Riverson can't see her face but he can feel her fury, her agony, her pride; it's all his own as well. "Seal this bastard back in the fucking sun, River. That's a command."

Riverson looks away, he no longer needs to follow the empress with his eyes, he knows her mind now and can feel her anger simmering in his soul alongside his own tremulous resolve. The weight of her memories rushes into him. It is beautiful, terrifying, and it makes him whole in a way that he hadn't known he was missing

And he doesn't have time for it. He looks up at Fabian. "Again," he says. "Kiss me again."

And this kiss isn't a question, it's a retort, a grand claim that even if the universe is beholden to monstrous forces, its greatest output is this tiny moment of human connection, of lust and its rallying heat.

It means loosening his grasp on the Feast, but Riverson knows now that he's found himself at the heart of a paradox: to regain control, he must cede it. So he confines his fears to the further part of his mind and allows himself to feel it—really *feel* it—when Fabian puts his hand up into his shirt and against the warm flesh of his uninjured flank. Riverson lets himself moan when Fabian climbs on top of him, strips off his sodden shirt, and presses down with the full weight of himself. Riverson reaches up, kisses his collarbone, and lets his fingers trail down Fabian's contracting stomach muscles. And River catalogs each of these moments in a semi-reverent trance: the taste of salt on Fabian's skin, the heat of him, the way his hair tickles when it falls across Riverson's face, the insistent throb where Fabian's crotch presses into his leg.

As Riverson's desires unfurl, the Feast shakes off its despondency. The primary note of the writhing mass becomes a desperation to connect. The kisses become furious, the touches imperative. Even Celestin, restrained as he is, seems adrift in the erotic haze, stiffness no longer in his posture alone.

Riverson is insistent, too. Fabian's hand works below both their waists, twinning their erections to each other as the men writhe, their mouths pressed together like the air is running low. Riverson knows the feeling that is building inside of him—he has a thorough understanding of every part of the human sexual response—yet he's genuinely surprised by how breathless he becomes as the feeling gains on him. He wants to tell Fabian as much, but the Null_Wolf's face is frozen between humor and pain, and…ecstasy?

"I'm close," Riverson says.

"I know," Fabian replies.

Their faces hover so close that any flicker or twinge could send them careening into each other. *Sex makes us ridiculous*, Riverson decides. It's his last coherent thought before the explosive sensation undermines his conscious mind.

And it is a magnificent orgasm.

In that moment, Riverson splits into two discrete beings: there is the part of him breathing hard as Fabian, grunting, paints his bare chest; there is also a part of him sitting across from the Rapacious in a white room. The chairs are wooden, simple, and there is nothing else.

The world-ender is wearing a crisp white suit against dark skin. His braided hair falls to one side; his head lolls as he regards Riverson.

"Apologies for the suddenness of this meeting. I found a quiet place in your mind for us to talk for a bit. Just us." The Rapacious licks his full lips, yawns. "Never, not once in the fullness of history has one of your foremothers subjected herself to the Feast. I'd be surprised if any of them had even considered it. And yet, here we are. You've made yourself a vessel for the same erotic impulse that you've used to exert control for the lifespan of your little galactic empire. How does it feel, Feast-Emperor?"

"Like I have a great deal to clean up."

The beast grins, scoots to the edge of his chair and shakes his head. His heavy lidded eyes are half-open. "Oh, I don't doubt that for a single moment. But I want to know how it feels, River. The sensation of it. You dragged yourself down to your animal core to save a collapsing house of cards. You risked losing all that meticulous control and gambled that a little sex could keep me in line. So, how did it *feel*?"

Riverson doesn't hesitate. "Glorious. And fuck you, by the way."

The Rapacious covers his left eye, wipes at it with the back of his hand like a sleepy child. "As fun as that would be, I'm so full of your sensations that I couldn't have another bite." He parts the fingers of the hand covering his eye and reveals that instead of iris and sclera there is now a void: cold, unyielding, endless. "Well, I could have just one more bite." He blinks and his eye is an eye again. "But I have to admit Riverson, Thirty-Second Feast-Emperor, that you have impressed me. So, I'll be good and go back to sleep for a bit, so you can play pretend-daddy to your other voracious parasites."

Riverson's impulse is to overturn the chair and scramble away from the beast's awful appetite, but he stays seated and upright. He will not flee again from this thing.

"We aren't done, you and I," the Rapacious says. "You've proved to be something…different than your staid and proper other selves. It may be time to renegotiate the boundaries of our arrangement. I'll be in touch." The Rapacious yawns so widely that Riverson sees his mouth full of countless terrible teeth.

And then Riverson snaps back into himself, his real, actual self. Fabian is sheepishly wiping at the emperor's chest with Riverson's own shirt. "Sorry," Fabian says. "I didn't expect…so much."

Riverson doesn't answer, he closes his eyes and tries to connect to the desperation and pain of the Feast. Instead, he finds that it has resumed its baseline hum. The terror and anxiety that cast such a pall over the Feast has abated and it has clicked back into its status quo—well, as close as can be expected after near annihilation.

When Riverson opens his eyes again, Fabian is sitting with knees to his chest and his arm thrown over them. He's still shirtless, and his body…

Riverson clears his throat. "Our situation is resolved for now. The Rapacious will leave us alone, I think."

"And all I had to do was masturbate the emperor. Imagine that," Fabian replies.

Riverson gives him a withering glare. "It's not too late to make good on the capital part of your capital crime. And keep in mind that our arrangement was purely for the sake of survival; please don't assume any increased intimacy."

Fabian looks at Riverson for a long time before responding. "Emperor, respectfully, you slaughtered thousands of my brothers with a gesture. I think it's safe to say that we aren't friends, whatever else this episode has made us." He stands, wincing as he puts his shirt back on, and incrementally shifts from Fabian back to the Null_Wolf, even if he leaves his cracked mask on the ground. "I'm glad our problem with the Rapacious is over, Emperor, because we have a great deal to talk about regarding the future of the empire."

Riverson levers himself up as well. "Indeed. I believe I have a solution to that matter."

Fabian narrows his eyes. "Oh?"

"But you're not going to like it."

"Oh."

DUE TO THE unceremonious consumption of the senior Corrected Center staff—those who weren't eviscerated by the Null_Wolf, anyway—several junior (i.e. surviving) members of the staff are "promoted" to manage the clusterfuck left in the wake of the Rapacious's attack and several notable betrayals. One of these lucky staff members is a gruff, but confident young woman named Siobhán who takes up Leeds's slate and begins hovering over Riverson's shoulder as if born to the job.

Nine soldiers from around the station are sent to the Feast Hall in order to stand around and pretend that if the Null_Wolf intended to take them apart they would offer a challenge. Having seen him in action, Riverson doesn't have these illusions. However, the presence of muscle is part of the tapestry of rule and having just bluffed his way through the survival of the galaxy, Riverson is not above impressions. Also, he can admit that he feels a bit more comfortable with their presence once he has Celestin and Leeds freed from their restraints.

The general of the Perpetual Front rubs his wrists. "I don't understand. You've won, Feast-Emperor. Why offer mercy now? What does it benefit you?"

Riverson doesn't answer him directly, instead he tilts his head over one shoulder and asks: "Siobhán, how many worlds do the Perpetual Front have bases on?"

His new assistant answers without looking down at her device. "One thousand four hundred and six, Emperor."

"Significant," Riverson says.

"I still don't—" Celestin begins, but Riverson isn't listening.

"Null_Wolf."

"O great Emperor, bearer of the finest cock in the galaxy?" Fabian replies.

Riverson gives him A Look. "How long before the rest of the Luperci comes to kill me again?"

Fabian's grin slips a little. "We would never..."

Another look.

Fabian inspects his fingernails. "Already en route, I'd imagine."

"And how might they be persuaded to relent?" Riverson asks.

"Well, you *could* cede the throne. If I were emperor, then we'd have gotten what we want, despite the notable sacrifice of my brothers, which—"

"Fine. It's yours," Riverson says.

Fabian continues. "—was significant. We could be convinced to be generous, spare you and your staff, of course. But...wait, *what* did you just say?"

Riverson explains. "Bloodlines are important to this empire. Important to the maintenance of the seal that traps the beast. The Luperci is a renewable resource that can ensure we don't run out of necessary blood."

"We're not a blood bank, Emperor!" Fabian says, objecting with his words and his eyebrows.

"Former emperor," Riverson corrects, moves on.

"At least I will be once I finish this. The Luperci will take power, but everything I've learned about your brotherhood suggests that you are preening, power-hungry, grasping sycophants. So, the Perpetual Front will be given a new mandate and expanded powers. Rather than colonizing the furthest reaches and making fascinating new enemies for us to fight, the Front's attentions will turn inward."

The general of the Perpetual Front blinks several times in a row, then snorts with the frankness of a dead man. "A sop you'll throw to the Front while sucking off the Luperci. Do you really think—"

Riverson talks over him. "There exists no body more well-positioned to give voice to the planets under the aegis of the Staghead Empire than the Front. Nor to correct the sins visited upon those people." Riverson regards Celestin, who appears to be evaluating his sincerity, looking for the trap. "General Celestin No-One, you've made it clear that you are from common stock. I hope you do not lose that touchstone as you are made the First Ambassador of the Front by imperial decree as my word is law. You will ensure the longevity of the planets that have been taken within the grasp of the empire, and should they so choose, secure their release from that grasp."

Celestin sniffs. "You're giving me a thankless task. The Luperci will work to stymy any attempts I make to weaken the empire you've just gifted them."

Riverson's rose-hued eyes are unblinking. "Consider it your punishment for having the gall to survive your assassination attempt. If you are expecting pity, you will find none."

"Nor do I expect it, Feast-Emperor." Celestin bows. Ever the soldier and dignified to the last. "I will serve."

Fabian laughs, shakes his head. "You've sold the house and torn out the gardens on your way out the door. You expect us to accept this? What reason could the Luperci possibly have to allow this desecration of our holy mission to expand the bounds of the Staghead Empire?"

"Would you like an *intact* empire, Null_Wolf? Or would you prefer I relax my grip on the Feast and allow the beast to take another bite of your shiny new toy? Don't mistake me," Riverson explains. "I am making *you* emperor, not one of your other pureblooded brothers, because you have seen the devastation firsthand; you know the horrors I can unleash if you don't treat fairly with me, or with the Front. And on the subject of brothers, you'll turn your order into something that better resembles the women, witches, saints, that created it."

The Null_Wolf's hand twitches at his side, brushes the steel of his weapon. Ultimately, his hand floats away from it and he smiles broadly. His voice drops low enough for just the emperor to hear. "We have witches too, River. We will work them day and night. One day, we'll figure out how to contain the beast without you and then we will take *everything* we deserve."

"So, until then…?" Riverson asks. He tries not to think about how sexy the Null_Wolf is when he's menacing.

Fabian grins. "Until then."

"So be it." Riverson looks over his shoulder. "Siobhán, make the announcement. And, I suppose, find him a crown."

Then Fabian Kikoytza, the incoming emperor of the Staghead Galaxy, approaches Celestin and extends a hand. "Well, Ambassador No-One. It sounds like we'll be working closely together until I can figure out how to get rid of you."

Celestin shakes it. "Or until I figure out how to rot this empire from within and come up with something better— something democratic, even."

Fabian laughs. "Democracy, as if such a thing could ever survive outside of a classroom."

Riverson leaves the men to their posturing to address Leeds, flanked by guards. The former First-Retainer looks serene, or at least at peace.

"Marvelous maneuvering, Emperor. Treating your allies and enemies the same, pitting them against each other to ensure a balance and threatening otherworldly retribution to keep the entire thing in check. Brava," Leeds says.

"Political ingenuity is aspirational, Leeds," says Riverson. "Had you kept faith you could have been a part of a new galactic order. Something a step toward equity. You could have helped guide it."

Leeds looks at Riverson and he knows the look: pity. "You still don't understand, Emperor. You make gestures toward order, toward the essential rightness of your actions, but can only stem the flood that will eventually purify us all. You think yourself the jailer of the beast, but you are fragile, and when you break, everything will wash away."

Riverson shivers. Leeds's gaze discomfits him— something beneath the zeal feels like portent. But Riverson has already steeled himself, so the next words come out easily and don't betray his rattled nerves. "Leeds, traitor to the throne, you and the other members of your cult are hereby banished to the furthest planets of my empire. Should any of you be detected close to this sun or the worlds that surround it, you will be executed on sight. This is my last decree as Feast-Emperor of the Staghead Empire and it is inviolable."

Leeds bows before the guards drag them away and as with Celestin's respectful gesture, it feels authentic, despite the gulf between them. Riverson feels the pull of something akin to sadness—belatedly he recognizes it as the weight of the crown he no longer wears.

EPILOGUE

THE
FLOOD

RIVERSON'S NEW TITLE is Conductor of the Feast and his imperial raiment has been replaced with simple robes of crimson and gold, which he wears open to the navel. He pads across the pathway at the center of the Feast Hall with bare feet and steps over a couple vigorously humping and muttering words to each other that are considered illegal on some worlds. He makes his way toward the edge of the dais, and stares through the protective coating of the hall's dome into the swirling chaos of the sun; it's a personal ritual that he completes regularly, to remind himself what's at stake in this room.

There is no longer a formal hierarchy within the Corrected Center. Those inclined to join the Feast do so out of a love of revelry and a dedication to the work of subverting the beast's will, rather than the desire to place themselves nearer to the throne. Or at least that's what Riverson would like to believe, but he knows there are a fair share of starfuckers who desire nothing more than to slip between the thighs of the former emperor. He knows because he's fucked them, and been fucked by them. After all, he's not a priest.

As he walks toward the sunward-edge of the dais, a familiar face turns toward him, it's practically his own.

"You woke late, descendant. Indolence appears to suit you," she says.

"Please, Lemia. Is it possible to pass a pleasant day with you?" Riverson replies.

She frowns; it's her natural state.

Riverson didn't mean to permanently incarnate the ghost of the Feast-Empress, but joining the Feast himself has had…unintended consequences. As stiff and foreboding as the Feast-Empress is, she has softened somewhat toward Riverson, even going so far as to share her name. Although it still seems too soft on the tongue for the intractable woman.

"Indeed," says the other voice.

The Rapacious sits with her legs spread, thrice-pierced genitals bared for all to see. And all *can* see, because both the Feast-Empress and the Rapacious have escaped the bounds of Riverson's mind to take up permanent residence aboard the Corrected Center. The participants of the Feast were alarmed at first, but phantasms borne by the mind of their leader apparently fell within acceptable range of the uncanny; after a few days, this minor disturbance to the Feast became just another feature of its strangenesses.

However, it was not strange, or at least not uncommon, in the new order of the Feast for Riverson to look out into the fracas and see the thick thighs of a Front lieutenant wrapped around the head of a freshly inducted initiate of the Luperci, clearly having the time of her life. Bitter rivals united in a temporary, explosive truce. Riverson makes it clear that all are to be welcome, even the spies that the emperor regularly sends to check-in on the proceedings. More than once, the Feast-Conductor has been personally apologized to by a sheepish member of the newly installed imperial court for doubting the legitimacy of his work. Of course, this is after an orgasm or five. The kind of pleasure that the Feast offers can make anyone feel generous with their praise. They don't even seem to mind the shapeshifting monster watching them fuck and be fucked.

But for Riverson himself, it took longer to accept the presence of the dread beast. Its existence seemed to suggest that the Rapacious had lied about going to sleep within the sun. However, the Feast-Conductor soon learned that this thing he had manifested was not exactly the Rapacious, at least not the worst of it.

"Lemia, dear. You have been dragged out of the clutches of death, why not enjoy your time?" says the Rapacious, or its echo.

"Do you think I take my behavioral cues from a psychic fragment of a chained wyrm?" Lemia asks the Rapacious pointedly. "If I need your counsel, beast, I will throw myself into the sun and ask you myself. The *real* you."

"I'll keep it warm for you, darling," the Rapacious answers.

She looks at Riverson and narrows her eyes. "It's worse than it was a few weeks ago. You're changing too quickly."

Riverson knows what she means, but waves off her concern. "I'm in control; I can maneuver them now."

"They should not *exist*," she says, seething.

She refers to the other consequence. So far the members of the Feast have been unable to perceive it, but Riverson has begun projecting tendrils of pulsing, silky pink light. The psychic tendrils float from within his body in moments of arousal; unlike the destructive power of the Rapacious, they do not take life indiscriminately. Instead they seem to amplify the desire of those they touch, stoking their passions and driving them to greater heights.

At least, they have so far.

"It is another attempt to pervert the power that keeps the beast chained," Lemia says.

The Rapacious shrugs. "Then end yourself and see what the river sends us next. Maybe all this is temporary, a fluke. Maybe my power over you will dissipate in an instant."

"No," says Riverson and Lemia at the same time. They have an eerie habit of doing so, especially when it comes to this subject.

Neither Riverson nor his forebear can predict what will happen once he dies. The flow of the river—so predictable for so many iterations—has changed, and until they understand the nature of that change, Riverson's survival is crucial. So, it's somewhat inconvenient that he's made enemies of the powerful Luperci and has a representative of the Rapacious living aboard his station. Still, Riverson tries not to worry about things he can't control, and there is much he can't control.

"I'll handle this," Riverson says. "I have so far."

Naturally, Lemia frowns. The Rapacious says nothing, just stares, and touches herself, and smiles.